CW01192619

The Last Night at the Star Dome Lounge

The Last Night at the Star Dome Lounge

M. R. Carey

THE LAST NIGHT
AT THE STAR DOME LOUNGE
Copyright M.R. Carey © 2022

Cover Art
Copyright Ario Anindito © 2022

Introduction
Copyright Marie O'Regan © 2022

This hardcover edition is published in October 2022 by Absinthe Books, an imprint of PS Publishing Ltd, by arrangement with the author. All rights reserved by the author.

The right of M.R. Carey to be identified as Author of this Work has been asserted by him in accordance with the Copyright, Designs & Patents Act 1988.

This book is a work of fiction. Names, characters, places and incidents either are products of the author's imagination or are used fictitiously. Any resemblance to actual events or locales or persons, living or dead, is entirely coincidental.

ISBNs
978-1-78636-871-3
978-1-78636-870-6 (signed edition)

Design & Layout by Michael Smith
Printed and bound in England by TJ Books

ABSINTHE BOOKS
PS Publishing | Grosvenor House
1 New Road Hornsea, HU18 1PG | United Kingdom

editor@pspublishing.co.uk | www.pspublishing.co.uk

INTRODUCTION

I WAS DELIGHTED WHEN MIKE (M.R.) CAREY AGREED TO WRITE a novella for Absinthe Books; I've been a huge fan of his writing for a long time. From the Felix Castor series to now (*Someone Like Me* is one of my favourite books), there's been so much to enjoy, whether in the form of novels like *Girl With All the Gifts*, *Fellside* or the above-mentioned Castor books and *Someone Like Me*; graphic novels such as *The Unwritten*, *The Dollhouse Family*, or working in universes such as Lucifer and X-Men; or even screenplays—Mike was nominated for a BAFTA for Best Newcomer for his screenplay adapting *The Girl With all the Gifts*.

I think we've established I'm a fan, so when he agreed to write a novella I knew we were in for a treat. The fact he's a great friend was a welcome bonus; I first met Mike at one of the earliest Alt. Fiction events in Derby, and he and his wife Lin have become very good friends of Paul's and mine in the years following that event, as have his children in more recent years. They were kind enough to volunteer at the convention Paul, another friend Alex Davis, and I ran earlier this year, ChillerCon UK, and their help was invaluable. His only guidelines were that the story had to contain some speculative element; other than that, everything was entirely up to him. And I couldn't wait to see what he came up with.

With *The Last Night at the Star Dome Lounge*, Mike has delivered a sweet-weird story that will in turn charm and surprise the reader. Fain has inherited Ocean View, a boarding house in Hove Harbour from her late mother, who's still hanging around to offer advice where needed and generally keep an eye on the place—to tell you any more than that would ruin the story for you, so I'll let you find out for yourself. Suffice to say Mike has written a tale of magic, and love, and created a place you won't forget in a hurry. So turn the page and begin your visit to Hove Harbour and *The Last Night at the Star Dome Lounge*.

It's going to be a night to remember.

—Marie O'Regan
Derbyshire, June 2022

THE LAST NIGHT AT THE STAR DOME LOUNGE

To my family
You know this house

FAIN STARTS EVERY DAY BY THROWING HER KNIFE AT THE WALL of her bedroom.

It used to be her mother's knife, a fearsome thing with an ebony handle nicely shaped to her left hand and an edge that never seems to wear away. It used to be her mother's wall too, come to that, but Cass Cabordet has been dead these three years and nobody this side of Hell knows where Joseph is, so now it's Fain's wall and Fain's knife because she was the only one left around to inherit them.

She's not actually aiming at the wall when she throws. The target is a circular cross-section from an old alder stump that Cass dug up in a neighbour's garden. She had a vague idea of making the rough-hewn disc into a trivet but death intervened. Fain has it propped up on a shelf that formerly held a potted geranium. When she hits the block in or around dead centre it falls neatly back onto the shelf, to Fain's intense satisfaction. If she snags an edge it crashes to the floor and startles Mr Overton in the room below, sometimes drawing a yelp of surprise and dismay that Fain can hear through the floorboards. If she hits the wall the knife sinks into the lath and plaster up to its hilt, doing the wall no good at all. At some point she'll have to break into her meagre savings and pay a plasterer to come and repair all the holes she's made, but she can never quite bring herself to do it. She's sure to miss again at some point, and it would be a shame to waste the money.

In any case, she doesn't really mind that she's degrading the fabric of the house. There are days when she feels the house isn't doing much good for hers.

Fain's day has a shape that doesn't vary. The shape is this.

She wakes around a minute before seven, just in time to put her finger between the hammer and the bell on her alarm clock. The hammer raps repeatedly against her nail, a pressure that almost becomes a pain, which helps to wake her up.

She sits up, takes the knife and makes her shot. She doesn't retrieve the knife or pick up the block if it's fallen. It's enough to note where she hit or by how many inches she missed. She doesn't miss very often these days, which is gratifying.

Why did Cass Cabordet have a knife balanced for throwing? Fain has asked many times and received many answers, all of them teasing and ridiculous. Cass wasn't given to violence or the bluster and blazon of weapons, but she was always in her quiet way a woman who could take care of herself in difficult situations. Fain assumes the knife is a last resort that fortunately never needed to be used.

Once she's made the throw she rises from the bed that used to be her mother's and (much longer ago) her father's too, the old springs under her strumming their own dawn chorus, and walks to the window. She likes to stand there naked and say good morning to the sea and sky. It's good to start the day with beauty, Fain thinks, since so much of it will be taken up with dull plodding of one sort or another.

She washes and dresses and goes downstairs to lay out breakfast. Usually Mr Henbosch will already be in the kitchen, waiting, and he will make one of two jokes depending on whether Fain arrives before 7.15 or after. The before 7.15 joke is "So how many worms did you catch, Miss early bird?" The after 7.15 joke is "Why if it isn't the late Miss Josephine Cabordet!" Either joke is guaranteed to get a big laugh supplied by Mr

Henbosch himself. To be fair, he's an appreciative audience for other people's jokes too, not just for his own.

All four of the live-in boarders take breakfast (though only the two gentlemen sit for dinner). Fain puts out two fresh loaves, one with seeds and one without, butter, jam and cheese. Usually the jam is damson and the cheese is Slipcote, but at weekends it might be gooseberry and Brighton Blue. There is tea from an urn, and hot porridge oats simmering if any of the boarders have put in a request the night before.

Breakfast is stressful, because Mr Overton disapproves of Mrs Simons and dislikes sharing a table with her. He suspects her—rightly—of offering some of her clients sexual services along with her prognostications, and he believes it's somewhat scandalous for her to rub shoulders and other body parts with ordinary, decent people. He has asked Fain more than once, obliquely but with a certain nudging urgency, what her thoughts are on the subject of immoral earnings (they tend to be more reliable than the other kind, is Fain's considered opinion). Mr Overton is also diffident around the other female boarder, Rosie Flack, for reasons that most likely relate to her forthright language. When Rosie swears, she swears like a sailor on his third night of shore leave.

Mr Overton is a widower, a retiree and an amateur collector of postage stamps and postal history. He was a military man back in the day but he doesn't have much to say about that period in his life. The only visible sign of it, which Fain sees when she goes into his room to empty the wastebasket and swap out the bedsheets, is his Webley-Fosbury service revolver in its case on the bedside table, accompanied by two boxes of ammunition stamped with the seal of the Royal Ordnance Factory at Radway Green.

Mr Overton's height would be impressive if it were not for his stooped shoulders. Certainly his legs are the longest Fain has ever seen attached to a human frame. His wife, Margaret, died more than twenty years ago, and it's highly unlikely that he's had anyone in his bed since. Fain has considered suggesting that Mr Overton ask Mrs Simons for a reading, but he would probably have some sort of hysterical episode at the mere thought and in any case Mrs S would almost certainly refuse. She's a woman of good sense and she would see the potential complications from a mile off.

Mrs Simons is an austere woman in her forties with prematurely grey hair and aquiline features. She looks much more like a university professor or a lawyer than a spirit medium. Nonetheless she tells fortunes at fixed rates using a device she calls a bone abacus. She does her readings on a green baize cloth intended for a bridge table, on which she has drawn in black marker several zones and divisions with esoteric names such as THE UNREMEMBERED and FORTUNE'S FIELD. Across this cloth she first brandishes and then flings down three dozen bones which she says are all from different species of animal, including many now extinct. One of them she claims is a fragment of an angel's scapula, and another the *baculum* or penile bone of a Sumatran tiger. As for the sex, she enjoys it a great deal but she is not indiscriminate. She just finds it useful sometimes as a means of obtaining a sharper focus on her subject. Usually she enfolds it into the same overall price, but she will charge extra if she feels it's been a chore.

Mrs Simons read for Fain once, and told her she would one day cut the cord so her lover could be born. Fain was nonplussed. "Am I supposed to fall in love with a new-born baby then, Anna-Louise?" she asked Mrs S. "Oh no, dear," Mrs Simons assured her. "In fact I get the sense that it's someone quite a bit older than you. The cord you cut isn't an umbilical. It's more like a noose or something. I'm not sure. The bones are being coy with me today."

Mr Henbosch is an inspector for the water board, and has no feelings one way or the other about what other people do for a living unless he can dredge up a pun from it. "I work for the water board—and I do get very *bored* with *water* sometimes." And so on. A propos of Mrs Simons' more unorthodox forms of divination he once tried to build a joke around for*tunes* and fore*play*. Mrs S told him she would describe the moment of his own death to him if he didn't stop, and he has left the subject alone since.

Puns are Mr Henbosch's pastime, but practical jokes are his passion. As a result he lives under strict interdiction. There are to be no pails of water set over doors, no joy buzzers or charcoal soaps, no spring-loaded snakes in bottled preserves or flowers that spray water in the eyes of the unwary. Fain doesn't want to rain on parades or poop on parties but in this, and this only, she's a utilitarian. The greatest good for the greatest number lies in Mr Henbosch only expressing his sense of humour in words. Mr Henbosch pines but does not complain. Fain suspects that one day he will break the ban in some spectacular way. Until that day an uneasy truce reigns.

And Rosie Flack? Rosie is a doctor at the Southern Coastal Infirmary. She could afford far better accommodation, but she took her room a long time ago when she was a lowly intern and she has never found a reason to leave. She likes that she can walk to work. She likes, too, that the rent is reasonable and the foaming, freshening sea stands squarely in her window every morning. Most of all she likes the house itself. She's told Fain it has a welcoming atmosphere, a cosiness. She feels at home there.

After breakfast Fain does a load or two of laundry. Rosie takes care of her own washing, just as she cooks her own evening meal. Fain washes for the other three boarders and for several neighbours, charging four pounds a week. It's not a job she enjoys but she knows it's important to get started early, especially on cold days when the clothes will need that much longer to dry.

When the wash is wrung and hung she goes to market, buying whatever she needs for that evening's dinner. Sometimes she extends the walk down to the harbour so she can see what ships are in. A large vessel in port will sometimes translate into overnight boarders, and they can often trickle in quite late after the bars and brothels have thrown them out. It's worth keeping the front door unlocked if there's a chance of filling one or two of the house's empty rooms for a night or two.

Fain's afternoons are taken up with more washing and with whatever cleaning and minor repair work is needed around the house. There's always enough to fill the time until she has to start cooking dinner. The cooking is companionable because she shares the oversized range with the women boarders, swapping bawdy jokes with them while she throws together a stew or a casserole for the menfolk. The evening meal itself, though, is mostly a hopeless case. Mr Henbosch essays a joke. Mr Overton, who doesn't get the joke, requires an explanation. Mr Henbosch, who doesn't know how to explain why a thing is funny (it just *is*) just repeats the joke instead of expounding it and laughs a little louder at the end. This cycle can easily go through three or four repetitions. Rosie and Mrs Simons eat in their room, and Fain doesn't blame them one bit.

After washing up from dinner and stowing any leftovers in the cold store Fain retires to her own room on the second floor. It's quiet up there, except for when Mr Henbosch plays his flute or one of Mrs Simon's clients reacts vociferously to a reading or else to her caresses. Fain reads a book, or adds another row or two to the tapestry reproduction of Almagestri's "Birth of the Muses" that her mother was working on when she died. Cass Cabordet watches from the mantelpiece and chides her when she gets it wrong. *You have to tamp it down harder than that, Jo!* she'll say, or *That thread is meant to be cadmium lemon, not hansa!*

"Come and take the comb yourself if you don't like it," Fain mutters under her breath. Of course her mother can't do that, being just a pound or two of fine ash in a stoppered jar, so it's a bit of a cheap shot, but it's hard sometimes to be supervised in your leisure time as though you're still a child. Fain hasn't thought of herself as a child for a long time. She hasn't thought of herself as a Jo either. Joe-zuh-fain was how her name was pronounced by an American naval rating she spent a night with a few years back. Just the one night, but she liked the sound of her name in his mouth (liked his mouth for other reasons too) and she kept a part of it for old times' sake.

Old times. Yes, there were a fair few of those. *It wasn't like this in my day*, Cass says often and often. *We were all so happy. Weren't we happy, Jo? You can't say we weren't!*

In Cass's and her husband Joseph's day the whole house—not to mention the wondrous Star Dome Lounge—belonged to the family, and an ever-changing menagerie of friends and acquaintances and hangers-on rotated through the extra rooms with no questions asked. Fain remembers the parties, both at the Star Dome and in the house proper, the men in their fine suits and the jewelled, sparkling women. She loved their dresses, their hats, the dazzling colours and flamboyant patterns that made them look like exotic flowers raised in some magical greenhouse.

There was never any need to take in boarders in those times because Cass's magic and Joseph's music brought in enough money to let them live in some style. Wine at table, evenings at the Star Dome, a cinema outing from time to time. They dined on meat and slept in velvet, as Joseph was wont to say.

But Joseph found softer sheets somewhere else. He ran away with a long-legged clarinettist. She had tried out for the Star Dome, played off-key and didn't get the gig, but obviously something about her had struck a chord with Joseph nonetheless. "Fuck him, then," Cass said. "We're fine without him, Jo." Or in other moods "He'll come back when he's tired of her. He knows that what he's got with us is better." Fain was only eleven at the time and still hanging doggedly onto that *Jo* as if it was a sheet anchor, but she knew in her innermost heart that neither of those things was true. Joseph wasn't ever coming home, and all three of them were very much the poorer for it. That was the last night the Star Dome ever opened. Well, the last night for a very long while.

But Cass didn't lie down under the blows of fate. She still had her magic, and in Hove Harbour magic has always been a respectable way to earn a living. There are parts of England where that isn't true—where witches are ducked, demons legally hunted and seers put to hard question as if this were still the Middle Ages. There are places where instead of leaving out milk for the fair folk people catch them in traps and throw them into furnaces. In London, where everything is modern and scientific and the rational consensus binds like iron, magic can't even find a purchase. The people's hearts are so closed to it that it melts away before it can form. Perhaps all the world will be like that some day, but for now there are pockets where the old ways go on in all their muddled, hectic glory and Hove Harbour—thankfully!—is one of them.

Cass Cabordet was a witch of some considerable power, but she had put most of her magic into one weaving a long time ago and she didn't choose to call it back. Minor charms were her speciality. At the Star Dome, if the evening was off to a slow start, she used to weave small illusions of couples dancing to encourage the more bashful diners to get up on the floor and join them. She also charmed the nets of fishing yawls so the fish would fill them and the window displays of local shops to add allure to their merchandise.

To leaven out this income Cass took lovers, carefully chosen for their solvency and their generous natures. Whether any hexing was involved on that side of the equation was a thing she was never prepared to discuss. "Men sometimes need to be told what they want," was all she would say to Fain. "Your father is a fine example there. Never did manage to work it out, poor dear. I only hope he's happy, wherever he is."

That part was a lie. Cass sent Joseph bad dreams on the first and last Friday of every month, and when she had her period she sent him the cramps that came with it. She was desirous that her errant husband should remember her from time to time, fondly or otherwise.

When the cancer began to grow in her, almost the first sign of it was that her magic faltered. Magic is of the whole body, she had always said. When the body's out of tune, there's no way to strike up a song from it. She succumbed quickly. It was three months to the day from first diagnosis to last rites. Fain suspects that her mother arranged it this way, made a conscious choice. She was always inclined to be brisk and no-nonsense about impending misfortune. Lance the boil, was one of her many mottos. Most likely she used what was left of her power to progress the disease to its crisis as quickly as she could.

And after the cremation she came home, her spirit taking up residence in the cheap and frankly ugly white ceramic urn that contains her mortal remains. Fain is happy for the most part to have her company, but she couldn't quite keep herself—when Cass first manifested—from picking at the logic of it.

"You do know that a cremated body leaves behind up to six or seven pounds of ash?"

Ooh! Did Rosie tell you that?

"And at a rough guess that jar is holding less than half a pound of you."

So?

"So, is the bulk of your ghost somewhere else, Mum?"

I don't think so, love. I didn't come here because I was attached to the ash. I came because I wanted to be here. Here in the house, with you.

"Oh." Fain thought about this. About having her mother's disembodied spirit as a permanent fixture in her bedroom. "Thanks," she said tactfully. "That's really nice."

In practice there has been an upside and a downside. Cass's presence doesn't impinge on her privacy as much as she had feared. When she has anyone staying over she puts the urn down in the parlour. Mrs Simons chats to Cass if she has space in between readings, and if not there's the radio to listen to and the neighbours to spy on. Cass doesn't complain.

On the other hand: *here in the house, with you.*

What if Fain wanted to go elsewhere? What if she had her own plans? It's not that she hates being the landlady of a boarding house, or settling down in the tiny seaside resort where she grew up. It's more that she never got to see what else was out there. If she made a choice, she made it without sampling the alternatives. And perhaps a choice on her part wasn't really required in the first place. Some things just happen.

That's it, anyway. That's the wobbly but workable *status quo* of the Ocean View boarding house. But it won't last.

Nothing does.

※

Mr Overton is the first to see it. This is mostly because his room (first-floor back, seaward side) lacks an *en suite* bathroom. When he's caught short in the middle of the night, which is not seldom, he has to get out of bed, leave his room and venture across the moonlit wasteland of the first-floor landing to the toilet. Along the way he passes two doors, the first leading to room 2B (first-floor back, landward) and the second to a linen closet.

But tonight, when he feels the over-full sensation in his bladder and surrenders as he must to its burgeoning insistence, is different from all the nights that have gone before. He crosses the narrow strip of carpet, avoids the creaking floorboard, then slows to a stop with his hand on the handle of the toilet door, trying to bring to the forefront of his mind the impression of strangeness and standing-out-like-a-sore-thumbness that has just struck him.

Something is out of place. Something is there that should not be there, an extraneous item in a count that always comes out the same. Mr Overton turns his head, warily and with some trepidation. He doesn't like this. It's two in the morning and he's the only one awake, an inauspicious starting point for any encounter. But there is nobody lurking in the shadows in the corner furthest from the window, nobody (except the man in the moon) peering in through the window itself, nobody looking down on him from the landing above.

Then he sees it.

The door.

In between room 2B and the linen closet there is a door that to Mr Overton's certain knowledge has never been there before tonight.

It looks innocuous enough, except that it's different even at first glance from the ones on either side of it. It's dark wood with a high varnish, and the handle and doorknob are of black wrought iron instead of wood turned on a lathe. It has four inset panels, two larger ones above and two slightly smaller ones below, the ratio being approximately 60:40. The lintel is a narrow shelf suitable for a vase or small ornament but currently unoccupied, supported by two voluted uprights. This door furniture is all painted in what was once brilliant white and is still one of those two things, though with occasional bare spots where the accidents of time and through-traffic have chipped the paint away.

Mr Overton stares at the door, unable to parse its presence there on any level at all. Perhaps he is dreaming. It has happened before that the demands of his full bladder have failed to wake him in time and he has dreamed an excursion to the toilet that has not in fact taken place. Those dreams ended in catastrophe. On this occasion, though, he still feels the urgent pressure from the region below his waist. It's enough to convince him that he is awake and that what he is seeing is real.

He hurries to the toilet and does what he needs to do. The normality of it is reassuring. But when he ventures out onto the landing again the door is still there. And now—as if its being there wasn't bad enough in itself—it's ajar.

The moment has cast its own sickly spell. Mr Overton retraces his steps until he's standing in front of the door, tiptoeing in his slippers as if it's some timid beast and he's afraid of startling it. The gap between the jamb and the door itself is a vertical strip of deeper dark in the already murky hallway. The moonlight is no help to him here.

"Hello?" he says, in a voice that's just a little higher than a whisper. "Is there someone there?" When no answer comes he reaches out and touches the door with the tip of one finger.

It opens, not as though he has pushed it but as though his touch has prompted it to extend an invitation. As though the door is acknowledging him and ushering him inside. But only a madman would walk through a strange door in the middle of the night with nobody nearby to go in after him if it means him harm.

He goes inside. He does not know why, and he is mystified by the fact of his own feet moving him forward, but there it is. He takes a single step, through the open door and across the threshold. He stands in the dark, breathing shallow and tremulous breaths, listening for any movement.

"Hello?" he says again. Still no answer.

It's almost a universal law that there should be a light switch just inside any room on the opposite side of the doorway from the door's hinges, so that anyone entering can immediately enjoy the luxury of seeing where they're going. Mr Overton gropes for a switch, doesn't find one.

But a moment later—again, as if the room has recognised his need and wants to answer it—the light goes on. No, not the light but the lights, plural. The room is large and rectangular, with the door on one of its shorter sides. It's long enough to accommodate three ceiling lights all in a row. There are sconced uplighters at various points along the walls. Also there are ornate bronze strip-lights on the desks that have been arranged in two neat rows down the entire length of the room. The walls are panelled in dark oak. There are portraits of serious-looking men with stiff, high collars.

There is no sign of anyone in the room apart from Mr Overton himself, but there is another door at the far end, also ajar. This, Mr Overton immediately apprehends, is not possible. The room itself is impossible, already too long to fit within the footprint of the boarding house's foundations. That there could be a further room beyond, lying in the same line, is clearly absurd.

"Look here now," Mr Overton says, as if he is about to take issue with the fabric of reality. But anything further he might have said is lost to time and chance as he sees what's on the desks. Underneath every one of those strip-lights is a stamp album.

For Mr Overton, postage stamps have been a passion for longer than any other enthusiasm he has known—ante-dating by several years the sexual fantasies he entertained in adolescence. In fact they furnished many of those fantasies. His most intense erotic dream (at age fifteen) was of a girl in his class at school licking stamps and pasting them directly into his *Rest Of the World* collection without using stamp hinges, the transgression as thrilling as the symbolism was blatant.

This is foolish! he thinks now, but he shuffles across to the nearest album anyway. It sits there in its own little spotlight of pooled radiance, brazenly inviting. Mr Overton lifts the cover and throws the album open.

Inside, positioned dead centre on the page, is a Labuan 1892 6 cent on 8 cent stock, Mauve, surcharged in red, inverted (with no dot at lower left). It stands alone, as it should. What, after all, would you put next to it?

"Oh!" Mr Overton exclaims softly.

He turns the page. The verso is blank. On its right-hand neighbour, a Hawaiian Missionaries cover from 1851, with a 2-cent, a 3-cent and two 5-cent stamps. There are two cancellations, both very clear, which read

HONOLULU OCT 4 US POSTAGE PAID. One of the 5-cent stamps is in the variant state, blue with purple border rather than blue throughout.

Mr Overton does not say "oh!" again. He does not say anything. He only clicks his tongue, as if words are trying to form but evaporating in the heat of his wonder and desire. He turns page after page and sweet merciful Jesus, the treasures he sees! Not treasures beyond imagining: this is the veriest stuff of his imaginings, somehow made flesh.

And there are twelve desks, but he realises now that there are shelves underneath each desk that hold more albums. This must be one of the foremost collections in the world.

He is roused from his reveries by a sound, a soft and barely audible creak. The door at the far end of the room has swung just a little wider, as if in a stray breeze (but there was no breeze). In the next room he can see another array of desks. There is also a sign above the door which he somehow failed to notice when he entered. It reads ST PIERRE AND MIQUELON DEFINITIVES.

A whole room, devoted to Mr Overton's favourite area of speciality! Oh, Newfoundland and Labrador are all well enough, but St Pierre and Miquelon had more lost and limited issues than both of those territories combined. It also had post offices that sprang up and then disappeared multiple times within the few hectic years of the border dispute between France and Canada. There are no words to describe the philatelic riches of that tiny, ephemeral province.

Mr Overton takes a step forward. Almost at the same time he sees a shadow move in that room beyond. It's very large, hump-shouldered and asymmetrical. Along with the movement comes a harsh scraping noise, as of some heavy mass being dragged across an unyielding substance.

The sound is stilled at once. Nothing moves now in the St Pierre and Miquelon room. Mr Overton, though, does move. This teetering tower of implausibilities suddenly reminds him of a much simpler mechanism consisting mainly of a spring and a spike and a piece of cheese. He backs toward the door. It's further away than he remembered. Surely he went no further than the first desk, a few feet at most. He takes one stumbling step after another, groping behind him for the open door.

The lights are fading. The shadows gather on the threshold of that second, inner room, then spill out into this one, the one Mr Overton is standing in, like a wave of ink.

Mr Overton's hand never does make contact with the door but he does find the doorway. He lurches out onto the landing with a curdling scream climbing his throat. Out of control of his own speed he hits the bannisters hard with all his weight on the backs of his heels. His long legs count against him, giving him a very high centre of gravity. He's going over.

But a hand stabs out of the darkness, grips his wrist—clamping down like a sprung trap—and hauls him back to safety. He collapses onto his knees, numbed with shock. The panic and the brush with death overwhelm his perceptions so that the world contracts to a black ball pulsing behind his eyes.

When he recovers his sense of who he is and where and why he finds that he is down on all fours on the hallway's threadbare carpet. Raising his eyes he sees first, full in the baleful moonlight, two legs. One is a leg of flesh and blood, shockingly bare, obviously female. The other, identical in its general proportions, is of some dark wood inlaid with strips of bronze. The bronze has chased designs on it, elaborate curlicues and flourishes.

Mr Overton's eyes continue their upward journey. The legs are attached to a woman, and the woman is naked. That is, she is naked except for a leather harness which attaches the wooden leg to the top of her thigh, looping just below the dark triangle of her pubic hair. Mr Overton's attention flicks away, comes back, flicks away again. He makes a bleating sound of astonishment, his senses overloaded. The woman is young, her skin pale, her hair midnight black. Her full breasts appear to have no nipples or areolae, her midriff no navel, although these details etch themselves in as soon as Mr Overton notices them. The woman's beauty, caught in the moon's white eye, is the cold magnificence of a funerary monument but it's still dazzling and disorienting.

"Are you all right?" she asks him. Her voice is very soft. It brushes the ear gently, as if it's on its way to somewhere else.

"I'm...yes," Mr Overton stammers. "Yes. I'm fine. Thank you." He removes his gaze once again from the vicinity of the woman's bare flesh. In doing so he sees that the supernumerary door has disappeared. There is only a stretch of unblemished plaster now between room 2B and the linen closet. "Who," Mr Overton gets the word out with some difficulty, "who are you?"

There's a silence that's long enough to be awkward, even in these extreme circumstances. "I'm...Mina," the woman says at last. "Yes. Mina, the new boarder."

Of course she is. Mina. Mina Sellicks, who arrived yesterday. No, not yesterday but several weeks ago. Mina, whose presence here is entirely to be expected because she lodges here. Mina, whose quiet manner instantly marks her out as a woman of sober disposition and spotless character. Mr Overton approves of Mina, even on the very slight acquaintance they've enjoyed so far. Which means—despite the providential timing of her appearance, that he's all the more shocked to find her wandering the house naked at all hours of the...

Not naked. In a nightgown, of course. A modest flannelette, coming a long way down below the knee. What was he thinking? The dark and his own mind, playing tricks on him. He feels a need to apologise, but that would mean confessing what he thought he saw. His tongue cleaves to the roof of his mouth.

"You should mind your step, Mr Overton," Mina tells him gravely. "The carpet is a little worn here. I expect that's why you tripped."

And he finds himself nodding in agreement, because the door that could not have existed can't be explained.

"Goodnight," Mina says. "I'll see you at breakfast."

"Yes," Mr Overton says. "Goodnight, Miss Sellicks."

He heads back to his room, 2A. When he looks behind him Mina is still standing in the same place on the landing. Perhaps she needs the bathroom too but doesn't wish to advertise the fact. It's only natural for a woman to want her privacy; there's nothing odd or worthy of remark about it.

Where is her room, though? Is it on this landing? It seems he ought to have remembered if it was, but he has no recollection at all.

He tucks himself up in bed again but sleep doesn't come. He keeps thinking about the shadow in that inner room—the shadow of something big and heavy that dragged itself with difficulty across the floor but still moved with surprising speed when it needed to.

He wonders what it wanted.

Something is different, Cass Cabordet frets. You left the door ajar, Fain, and something has crept in. I don't think it's anything good.

"Tell me again in the morning," Fain mumbles, and goes back to sleep. She was halfway through a dream, talking to an invisible friend about the nature of magical spaces. *Step outside the world,* her friend says, *and all at once you're contingent.*

Contingent on what? Fain asks. She's eager to learn. She knows her mother made spells that protruded a little way outside normal reality, but Cass would never talk to her about such things. Too dangerous, she said, even to a witch of her own power and experience. For a beginner, fraught with appalling dangers.

Not on what, on whom. In a magic that creates a new space, you're at the mercy of whoever's space it is. The creator can invent new rules, and you're obliged to obey them as if they were a little god. I myself was caught and tethered in a space of someone else's making. And then I became... but why am I telling you this?

I don't think you are, Fain says. *This happens to me sometimes, when I'm asleep. The future flows into the past, like a drain backing up. It's the one bit of the gift that came to me. My mother had much more of it, and so does Mrs Simons.*

Ah, comes the other voice, the voice of the imaginary friend. *What you have isn't of much use then, is it? Still, I'll watch out for it. It might find me out at some point, and I've good reason to hide. Wake up now. I've had enough of this.*

Fain wakes up, sits up and throws the knife. It's a miss, her first in forty-seven days. She is dismayed, utters a mild curse. That's a poor way to start the day.

Her mother tells her again as she washes and dresses, in a tone of grim foreboding: something has got into the house that doesn't belong there.

"Most likely a rat," Fain says. "I'll put some traps down."

It's not a rat. It's something wicked, Fain, and there's worse wickedness coming on behind. I don't like it, not one little bit. This island always had more than its fair share of monsters back in the day.

"The binders and breakers took most of them long ago, Mum." That's a half-truth though, and in any case it's not a thing that Fain cares to celebrate. Binders and breakers are brutal men plying a brutal trade. The nature of their work allows them exemption from criminal prosecution on any grounds apart from non-fulfilment of contract. They can literally get away with murder—because it's necessary to classify what they do as somehow being *different* from murder. Murder is the intentional killing of a human being: the entities the binders kill belong to races far older than humankind. This is why Hove Harbour has traditionally banned the practises of binding and breaking within the municipal limits. The indiscriminate slaughter of any race doesn't play well in this town and never has.

"Much more likely to be a gas leak than a monster," Fain concludes, with more confidence than she really feels.

There's no telling what it might be. All I know is I've got a bad feeling about it.

"I'll keep my eyes open, Mum, and my wits about me. I won't let anything creep up on me unawares."

Fain goes down to make breakfast. She finds Mr Henbosch in animated conversation with the new lodger, Miss Sellicks. So enchanted is he with the sweet-natured and engaging young woman that he forgets to make his usual jest. Fain's entrance (a minute after the 7.15 watershed) goes unremarked.

"But Mr Henbosch," Mina is saying, "what is it you do at the water board? I imagine it must be something very important."

"I'm a priest, Miss Sellicks," Mr Henbosch tells her.

"A priest?"

"Well my job title is purity inspector."

Mina laughs politely. She doesn't make more of the feeble joke than it is, but she also doesn't leave Mr Henbosch chuckling alone. Fain likes her for that. She puts out the bread and butter, the jam and the cheese and the rest of the breakfast paraphernalia with a lightness of heart in spite of her mother's doom-mongering. She's glad that Mina has come. The new lodger fills a hole that Fain hadn't even realised was there before, and she's no trouble at all. You'd hardly know she was in the room most of the time.

The others come down one by one and take their places. Mr Overton seems tired and strained and has nothing to say for himself. He tries hard not to look at Mina Sellicks at all, and whenever he accidentally catches her eye he blushes somewhere between carmine and permanent rose. The others rise one by one to go to work until finally he is alone at the table. He stares at his half-eaten porridge, unhappily stirring it with his spoon.

"Sleepless night, Mr O?" Fain asks him.

He doesn't answer.

Nightmares, Cass says from the mantelpiece up on the second floor. *Chewy ones, with some gristle to them. Whatever this thing is, it's touched him.*

Fain tries again. "Did you have bad dreams, Mr Overton?" He looks at her in puzzlement, as if she's spoken in a language he doesn't understand. "I don't think the postage was right," he says after a long pause.

Fain blinks. "I'm sorry?"

"There would have been ship fees as well as postal fees. Fifteen cents wouldn't have got a letter all the way from Hawaii to San Francisco." In response to Fain's blank stare Mr Overton shakes his head. "I'm sorry," he says. "I was miles away. I think I'll go for a lie down." He leaves the room with his shoulders hunched, like a man expecting an incoming missile from an unpredictable angle.

Fain folds her arms. "All right," she says. "This needs to stop."

※

But it doesn't stop. And that night it's Rosie's turn.

She comes home very late, when everyone else is already asleep. This being Friday Fain expects as much and has left the door unbolted. On Fridays, at the end of a hectic week and with the freedom of the shift change looming, it's the custom of Rosie and her friends—the young and the beautiful of the Hove Harbour Infirmary's thousand-strong staff—to repair to a pub called the Crown and Anchor and commandeer it for the evening. The publican at the Crown and Anchor is a retired surgeon: the towel doesn't go up for doctors, nurses or interns and the stay-behinds go on well past midnight.

Rosie is in a half-blissful, heavy-headed state, one of the many stations of the cross between blind drunk and woefully sober. As always, booze has made her hungry and she's looking forward very much indeed to a slice of Black Forest cake that she left sitting on the windowsill of her room so it would stay cold. Late as it is, she intends to eat at least half of the cake before she gives up on the day and slides, most likely still dressed, between the bed covers.

It takes her several tries to get her key and the lock to coincide. "Stay still!" she admonishes the lock. "Don't make me work for this." At last the lock complies. "Okay, then," Rosie says, "good." And she stumbles inside.

She mounts the stairs to her room—and since her room is at the very top of the building that means climbing the stairs until there are no more left to climb. Tonight she feels she must have missed her count: she's been ascending for a long time and she still hasn't reached the top.

When at last her foot, hovering over where the next step should be, comes down on level floor instead, she looks up and down and around in bleary puzzlement. What part of the house is this? It's a large space, high-ceilinged and echoing. The floor is of black and white tiles with a diamond sheen to them. There's a glass roof high above her, the full moon caught in one of its myriad panes. A conservatory! She's in a conservatory at the top of the house.

Even drunk, Rosie knows she's not dreaming. And if this isn't a dream then it's something else that lies outside her previous experience. In the middle of the moonlit space there is a table, and on the table is a cake— the largest piece of confectionery she has ever seen, by a long way. The moonlight turns everything to soot and chalk, so it's hard to tell, but the colossal gateau seems to be dark sponge interlaced with inch-thick layers of cream. There is a row of what look like large, luscious cherries arranged around the rim. It could be the parent glacier from which the tiny sliver waiting for her in her room was calved.

Rosie is pragmatic by nature. Although the cake's presence here is absolutely inexplicable it still looks like a very good one and she's inclined to taste it while she's here. After all she may never pass this way again. She approaches the table, seeing as she draws closer that there's a knife lying beside the cake, a single plate, a single folded napkin. Everything has been arranged for her convenience.

But just as she's about to pick up the knife she notices one further thing. This is not a whole cake after all, it's fifty per cent of a cake, perfectly bisected. The other half of the tray on which it rests is not only empty but perfectly clean, devoid of any crumbs or smears of cream to indicate where the vanished portions were quarried away. It's as though the cake was baked in a vast semi-circular tin, cast in this exact form.

She had meant to eat half of the slice of Black Forest cake that was in her room. The two concepts—the sweet, cream-filled cake and the idea of one *half* of it—had been sitting together at the forefront of her mind. Somebody or something has plucked those ideas from her cerebellum and given them back again in this oddly purblind way—a lure designed by an entity that clearly doesn't know why half a cake should be such an exciting prospect but is prepared (and equipped) to offer it up.

Rosie doesn't touch the cake, or the knife. She backs away warily from the table. Nothing moves in the room, but she's not alone. There's an area of deep shadow in one of the further corners that's not explicable by the angle of the moonlight and the contours of the walls. Something has gathered up all the shadows in the room and draped them in folds and pleats around itself. It's watching her now, remaining unrevealed.

"I see you," Rosie says, throwing her defiance against the dark in the absence of anything else. "I see you there."

"Eat the cake," the darkness whispers. "I made it for you."

"I don't want the cake," Rosie growls. She stands there, swaying a little because she's very, very drunk, and waits for the thing to advance on her. She doesn't want to turn her back because there's a pretty good chance that if it can whip up half a cake in the blink of an eye it can outpace her before she gets to the stairs, especially in her current condition. It's a horrible thought, the shadows expanding and rushing on her and her not seeing, taken in flight like a mouse scampering across the open floor towards a hole it won't ever reach.

The silence stretches to breaking point. Nothing breaks it.

"Demon, are you?" Rosie asks at last. "If you are, I'll set the binders on you. You won't even touch the ground, you monstrous thing."

More silence.

"I'm going now," Rosie says. "You stay there. You don't move." She wishes she'd grabbed that knife but she's not going back for it, not for all the cake in the world. Like Mr Overton the night before, she backs away one step at a time, retreating towards the stairs, scooting each foot to left and right as she brings it down in hopes of encountering the topmost riser. Given that even walking forward would be something of a challenge for her right then, it's amazing that she stays on her feet.

But she does. The stairs are there. The darkness still hasn't moved. She can do this.

"Don't you bloody well move," she warns the darkness again.

She takes it one slow, fumbling step at a time, eyes wide open, not even daring to blink. Now that she knows this flight of stairs is an anomaly, not part of the house at all in its normal, day-time guise, she can feel the strangeness of the wood she's walking on. Warm and slightly yielding, as if it's not wood at all but something alive that meets the soles of Rosie's feet with the best seeming it can muster.

When she's just a little over halfway down it seems to tire of the pretence. It shrugs massively and Rosie goes sprawling, the stairs rising up in a curved arc over her like a huge serpent rearing back to strike. She lands on her arse with a crash, throws up her arms to shield herself but the attack doesn't come. She's sitting on the hall carpet, legs splayed, staring at the bare wall in front of her.

"Rosie?" It's Fain's voice, calling from the floor below. She must have heard that crash. The whole house probably heard it, come to that. "Are you all right?"

Rosie opens her mouth to speak, to raise the alarm, but the staircase that should never have been there in the first place has up and gone. There's nothing to warn against, no proof she can point at to prove she's not seeing things. "I'm grand, Fain," she calls down, her voice steady in spite of the hammering of her heart and the wild sallies of her thoughts. "Just drunk, is all it is, and lost track of where my feet were coming down."

"Can I get you a glass of water? Or an aspirin?"

"I'm right as I am," Rosie says, though that's far from being the case.

"Okay. Goodnight, then."

"Goodnight."

Picking herself up, Rosie runs a hand over the unbroken plaster. It's cold to the touch. It would be, because it's a bitter night and this is the outer wall of the house.

So wherever she just was, it must have been somewhere else.

※

Fain has her usual chores to tend to the next day, but as she's cooking and washing up, shopping and scrubbing, dusting and polishing and repairing, her thoughts are on the strangeness that has come to roost in the house she knows so well.

She doesn't know the first thing about Rosie's ordeal of the night before but she was kept awake for several hours straight by her mother's grumbling and groaning from the mantel. Something dark, Cass kept saying. Something dark coming. Almost here. Oh! Oh! Oh! These premonitory twinges affect her like a kind of spiritual rheumatism, tormenting her and making her a torment to Fain in turn. She's very keen to bring this to a head so she can confront it and deal with it.

She makes opportunities to question each of the lodgers in turn. Has anything unusual happened to them lately, or have they noticed anything strange about the house? Mr Overton's description of his philatelic adventure is garbled and hard to follow, complicated by blushes and circumlocutions that she can't entirely fathom, but Rosie is forensic. "It was a fiend or a hobgad, Fain. And it tried to coax me in with cake, so it did, only it got the cake all wrong. It would have gone hard for me otherwise."

There's no longer any room for doubt. Some presence has come among them, and it seems to have an agenda that might threaten both the lodgers and the house.

As the sun dips toward the sea Fain finds a pocket of time that she can call her own and uses it to pay a visit to Mrs Simons. Seeing her on the doorstep Mrs Simons greets her with a warm smile. Then she sees that Fain is carrying her mother's urn and puts on a more sober expression. "Is this a social call, duck," she asks, "or are we consulting in a professional capacity?"

"The second one, Mrs S," Fain says. "That is, if you've the time. I hate to be a nuisance but Mum thinks we've got a visitor. One that's come without an invitation."

Mrs Simons opens the door wide and stands to one side. "Come along in," she says. "I've felt it myself, only I didn't know if it was ours or not. Sometimes it read as being next door. Other times I felt it right here in the midst of us. I didn't know what to think. Still don't, to be honest. But if we put our heads together I'm sure we can find it out."

Fain goes inside. Mrs Simons' room is the smallest in the house, but she's put mirrors on most of the walls to make the space seem bigger. Fain suspects it may also help to amplify the psychic hints and essences on which Mrs Simons bases her readings. There are ornaments on every surface, some exquisite and some tawdry. Most of them are gifts from grateful clients and Mrs Simons is punctilious about keeping them all on display. They're stores of positive emotions, she says: she can draw on them at need.

She tugs the curtains closed, removes some of the vases and ceramic shepherdesses from the small table and spreads her cloth. She'll be leading the session, since it's her space, which means the divination will rely mainly on the bone abacus. She spreads out the cloth and fetches the bones from their cupboard. She keeps them in a box made of black poisonwood given to her by a Greek sailor from the HS Leander who later drowned in the Caribbean. Hector Praxides his name was, and he was not her client but her lover. Mrs Simons believes with some fervour that Hector's spirit returned to the box when he died in order to be close to her; believes, too, that his silent communion with the bones has increased their potency and accuracy very greatly over the years.

The three take their places at the table, Fain and Mrs Simons and the urn at the two, six and ten o'clock positions respectively. Mrs Simons sets the box down on the table and pauses, fingertips touching the lid at all four corners, to let the *numen* settle on them. When she opens the box there is a sigh that comes from nowhere and everywhere.

She rolls the bones. They make a tiny, hollow clattering sound as they sprawl across the cloth. Some of them rock for a long time before they settle. The three women, two living and one dead, stare at the resulting pattern in silence for a long while.

"Danger," Mrs Simons says at last. "That much is clear, anyway."

"It comes from very close by." This from Fain. "Under our roof, as we thought."

And not complete, says Cass. *Not whole.*

"I'm getting that too," Mrs S agrees. "But I'm not sure if the incompleteness is of something left behind or of something changing and becoming. It could even be both." She squints, leaning down until the tip of her large nose almost touches the cloth. "Wait though," she says. "There's more, isn't there? Look at Fortune's Field." She waves her hand over the lower right quadrant of the cloth. "On the heels of this thing comes another thing. And it cloaks itself, which means it sees us looking and it's got some power. What's it doing, d'you think?"

Hunting, says Cass, in a tone that brooks no argument. *It's on the hunt.*

"Can we ask again, then?" Fain suggests. "If there are two things, not one, and if they're both dangerous, we need to know what we can expect. It's my job to keep my boarders safe from harm, so the more I know the better."

Mrs Simons frowns, considering. "Worth a try," she says. "But let's be careful with our words, shall we? The second cast tends to be looser than the first, not tighter. We'll need to coax a little if we want a plain answer."

She gathers the bones in her two hands, prepares to cast, but a very loud and very sudden knock on the door makes her hesitate. "Goodness!" she says. "Who can that be?" Fain is about to suggest that they ignore the knock and carry on, but she's too late. Mrs Simons, who is used to callers at all hours of the day, is already up and heading for the door. Opening it, she finds Mina standing on the doormat wearing an expression of polite concern.

"Good evening, Mrs Simons," Mina says in her quiet, pleasing voice. "I was sitting in my room reading when I felt the emanations from your spellcasting. May I ask if you're performing a divination? And if so, is it to investigate the strangeness that's come to the house these last few days and nights? If it is, may I offer my help? I have a lot of experience in that regard. I can foretell with cards or tea or simple touch of hands. I've even done it once or twice with barley grains tossed in a saucer, though I know that's country ways and not much used any more." She puts her hands together in a pantomime of beseeching. "I'd like so much to be of use to you. Unless you've already had your answer?"

"Not at all," Mrs Simons assures her. "You'd be very welcome, duck," she says. "I made one cast, but the answers were a bit on the fuzzy side. We were just about to go again."

She ushers Mina to the table, where she is cordially received by both of the Cabordet women. Fain in particular is delighted to see her newest lodger, and wonders why she didn't think of inviting her in the first place. She was aware as soon as she met Mina (how long ago was that now? It feels like ages!) that there was an aura of real power about her. She's exactly what they need. There's strength in a trinity, yes, but when you add another seer to the table any three of the four can become trine at any given moment. An augury that might seem opaque at first can suddenly yield up its secrets when viewed from a different angle. They'll sort this now, for sure.

"Better repeat your questions," Mrs Simons says, running her hand across the cloth to smooth it clean of any residual vibrations. "We'll start with you, Cassandra, as the oldest present. Spirits, attend. Bones that once were living, attend." She taps her thumb against the lid of the poisonwood box. "Hector, my sweet, attend and be their shepherd."

What's come among us? Cass demands.

"And what comes after?" Fain adds.

"What's their strength, and their desiring?" This from Mrs Simons.

"And where do they come from?" offers Mina. A curiously blunted question which surprises Fain at first. On reflection, though, there might be some advantage in knowing the origins of these impending threats. It might provide a clue to their nature if the other answers are muddied or contradictory.

But there are no other answers. After making her second cast Mrs Simons stares at the bones in perplexity. Fain is a second slower on the uptake, but then these are not her own tools. When she sees it she gasps. Against all the odds and against their mistress's expressed wishes, the bones have found a pattern that is completely random. It conveys no information at all.

Mrs Simons can find nothing to say. Her mouth is open in an O of perfect astonishment. When she does make a sound it's a wordless moan of dismay. She starts to tremble. Fain takes Mrs Simons' hand and squeezes it, offering commiseration and support. For a seer working with her own equipment, honed over thousands of readings, to get no response from the other side of the veil other than the echo of her own voice... it's worse than a snub. It's a catastrophe.

"I'll make some tea," Mina says tactfully, "and then we can try again."

But they don't. Hot tea heaped with three or four spoonfuls of sugar (Mina is rightly profligate) helps to restore Mrs Simons' equilibrium but she is afraid of pushing the bones and their resident ghosts too hard against the grain. If they've fallen silent it's for a reason, and it's best to let them find their voices again in their own time.

It's got a bad smell to it, all the same, Cass complains. *The spirits were talkative enough before. Someone's pressing on them. Stifling them. This is the very thing we're trying to find out about, doing its best to stop us.*

"What could it be, though?" Mina asks. "There were only the four of us when we sat down at the table, and there are only the four of us now."

"There were..." Fain says, but she checks Mina's arithmetic in her mind and finds no fault with it. She shakes her head to clear it. There's a weight sitting there. Whatever is pressing on the bones is pressing on her too. "Mrs Simons," she says, "I'm so sorry I brought this on you. Is there anything I can get you? I've gin down in the kitchen, and I think some brandy too." She doesn't say that they're left over from when her father still lived with them. Does booze go off? She's really not sure.

Perhaps it's fortunate that Mrs Simons says no thank you. She'd rather keep a clear head on her shoulders so she'll feel it when the channels open again. She has appointments arranged for later in the evening. She needs to rest and be alone, she says.

But when she picks up the poisonwood box to put it back in its cupboard she draws a ragged breath and sways a little on her feet. Fain steps in to support her, but she's not in danger of falling. She was just surprised by a contact. "It's Hector," she tells them. "It's my dearest Hector. He says..." she leans her head to the side, listening. "He says the power that spoiled our séance is very close. It had to be, to strike all the bones at once without any of them seeing where the blow came from. He says to trust only those we know and be wary of every stranger."

"I agree," Mina says emphatically. "You mustn't take in any new lodgers, Fain. Not until this thing is settled."

Fain raises an eyebrow at that. It's somewhat early in their acquaintance for Mina to be using her given name. The surprise fades quickly, though. Mina has never been one to stand on formalities with anyone: her nature is too open for that, too candid. And much as Fain hates to admit it, her advice is sound. The one thing they know for sure is that a second threat is coming in the wake of the first.

It would be very bad indeed to be caught between the two.

Two weeks go by, then three weeks, and still the axe doesn't fall. Fain's state of paranoid readiness, and that of the more magically adept lodgers, begins to slacken off a little. And then a little more.

They haven't forgotten that there's something among them that they didn't invite and don't want. They repeat the divination several times, with cards and tea leaves as well as bones, but despite the formidable talents the four of them bring to the table there is never an answer on the urgent question they're asking. Mrs Simons is still able to do divinations for her clients. The spirits' reticence is only on this one topic, and it comes suddenly each time as if someone has the power to gag them.

Obviously this is a very troubling thought, but at least there are no more night-time alarums. Then again, some of the residents have changed their routines. Mr Overton, for example, no longer ventures out to the toilet at night. He resorts to a chamber pot, which he empties and rinses out furtively before anyone else is awake. And Rosie hasn't had another early-hours bender since the one that ended in cake and chaos.

This is a strange time for all of them. On the one hand they're waiting, anxious, in a lull that doesn't feel peaceful. On the other, their daily lives go on very much as normal. Better than normal, in some ways,

Mina is a case in point. It's very hard now to remember a time when she wasn't around. It's not that she's a loud presence—quite the opposite—but she's so kind, so thoughtful. Either she reads other people's desires with astonishing insight or else a kind of serendipity, a kind of blessing, follows her wherever she goes.

"I thought you might like these," she says to Mr Henbosch, handing him a cardboard box. The box is heavy. It bears on its side the proud boast of H.J. Heinz & Co, 57 VARIETIES, and in a sense it lives up to that promise. Inside, instead of soup or ketchup, are several dozen old books, second-hand and well read. They are the works of the American humourist Stephen Leacock, whose comedic leanings depend very much on puns and clever word-play. Mr Henbosch is ecstatic.

To Rosie Flack Mina brings tequila, salt and lime. To Mr Overton an old, torn envelope whose stamp is a rare 1831 commemorative celebrating the cession of Berbice to the United Kingdom. To Mrs Simons the femur of a capuchin monkey. "I honestly don't know where it came from. I've been using it as a bookmark..."

And to Fain, in the fullness of time, she gives herself. Fain has never slept with a woman before. When Mina kisses her she is taken aback. "What's this?" she asks—a foolish question in the circumstances but she can't help herself.

"Is it not what you want?" Mina seems honestly and innocently surprised. "I thought I saw you looking at me. I mean, as if you were wondering."

Fain takes a moment to chase that down. Yes, she realises, she genuinely was checking out Mina's very graceful body, her very lovely face. It was an idle thought—or rather a number of idle thoughts over several days—probably brought on by the fact that she hasn't taken a man back to her room in more than a year.

"If you don't want to..." Mina says, eyes demurely downcast.

"No, I do," Fain assures her. "I just never have. I'm not sure I know how."

Mina's gaze flicks up to meets hers, and in the blink of an eye all that diffidence is gone. "It's easy," she promises with a grin that's pure mischief. "Come on, I'll show you."

In Fain's room Mina takes off her clothes without ceremony or self-consciousness. She unbuckles the straps on her wooden leg and props it up against the bedside table.

"The workmanship on this..." Fain says, running her fingers over the wood and metal. "It's a beautiful thing. Can I ask who made it?"

"I made it myself," Mina says. "I wouldn't trust anyone else with something I depend on so much." Her incomplete leg has the same proportions as the other, but ends in a perforated ridge of stippled flesh like the islands of a tiny archipelago. Mina massages the leg briskly with her strong, long-fingered hands. Her muscles ache, she says, after a day strapped into the harness. The pain is deep and dull, like a foreign substance that she has to squeeze out of her. It can take a while.

The sex is the best Fain has ever had. It's actually better than *all* the sex she's ever had if you were somehow to roll those many fucks and fumbles into a single experience. Mina sets every nerve in her body on fire, then puts out the conflagration with such a deluge of kisses, caresses and skilled manipulations that Fain is left feeling as though she's melted into a puddle and drained away into her bed's ancient, slightly spavined mattress.

"Was it good?" Mina asks afterwards, kissing Fain's belly.

"I think I've been wasting my life," Fain says, when she can say anything at all. "Yes, Mina, it was very good. It was wonderful."

"I'm glad." Mina settles beside her, head against the hollow of her shoulder. They fall asleep like that, and it feels like the most natural thing in the world. As though they've known each other for years and years and years.

But Fain's sleep is troubled. She dreams she's lost in her own house, wandering through room after room that shouldn't even be there, uncertain where her own room is, where she left her mother's urn, how to find the front door. She wakes with a bleary head and a fuzzy tongue, as if that glorious, unfeasible lovemaking has brought on a hangover.

The bed is empty. Mina has slipped away without disturbing her.

That first night is a template for all the nights that follow. Mina comes to Fain's room shortly after Fain retires. She knocks lightly on the door and Fain invites her in. It's just the two of them, on these occasions. Cass Cabordet's urn has found a temporary refuge in Mrs Simons' parlour, where the two older women talk late into the night about the vicissitudes of the modern world and lament in tandem at its foolishness.

Fain and Mina tumble, then they sleep in each other's arms. And at some point in the night Fain wakes to find herself alone.

Sometimes, between the sex and the sleep, she tries to initiate conversation, to prolong the moment of contact because this is starting to feel something like love and one thing that passes between lovers (or at least is meant to) is words.

"Where were you living," she asks, "before you came here?"

"It's not a place you ever heard of," Mina says. "And it's not a place you ever want to go to. I'm happier here. Happy with you." And her kisses get in the way of any other kind of intercourse.

Another time Fain asks about Mina's leg. Did she lose it in an accident or was she born that way? Mina thinks harder about that one, but after a while she shakes her head. "Neither," she says. "I was...yes, I used to be...not like this. But it was no accident that made me the way I am. It was a choice."

She seems unhappy, or perhaps angry. Fain embraces her and draws her close. "I didn't mean to pry, Mina," she says. "I'm sorry. I just want to know you better."

Mina snakes in her arms and pulls back to meet her gaze. Fain hasn't realised until this moment that Mina's eyes—which she vaguely thought were brown—are actually golden with brown flecks in them, like the stone called tiger's eye. They almost shine in the dim light of the bedside lamp. "Do you think if you know me better you'll like me more?" she asks.

"Yes," Fain says. "I hope so. Do you think I won't?"

Mina answers this question with another. "Why would anyone ever take the chance?"

There are other questions that are deflected in the same way. What does Mina do for a living? Where was she born? What does she like to do, besides making love? She never seems to go anywhere. During the day she'll disappear for three or four hours together, but then she'll suddenly be at Fain's side, helping with the cooking or the washing, without the door having opened or closed so presumably she was in the house the whole time.

Despite these mysteries, though, it's a happy time. The happiest Fain can remember since... well, since before her father left. She has grown used to thinking of the house as a millstone around her neck. She has worn self-pity like a bow in her hair, setting off an ensemble effect that she knew was tired and somewhat shabby. Love has landed in her life like a fox in a hen coop and sent all her thoughts scurrying in a thousand directions at once.

Because it *is* love. It's not just the kisses and the sweat and the grappling, exhilarating and novel though all those things are. Underneath them is a discovery and a realisation she wasn't ready for. And she knows even from her very limited experience that love brings abruptions, break points. For better or worse you don't come out of it the same. She has no idea what will arise from that, but she's ready to find out. She thinks. She thinks she is. Some of the time. At other moments she asks herself what she's doing, opening her heart to someone she barely even knows.

One night when she wakes alone, fretfulness and disquiet prompt her to get up and go looking for her errant lover. These are dangerous times, as they all know. She doesn't like the thought of Mina, who after all has a physical disability, wandering through the dark house and perhaps encountering the nameless thing that has somehow burrowed its way in.

She throws on her dressing gown and hurries out onto the landing. When she gets there she comes to an abrupt halt. The moon, still full-faced, looks down on her quietly from the skylight high above. Everything is still.

Fain is still too. She has realised, with blank astonishment, that she doesn't know which room is Mina's. How is that possible? There are nine rooms for lodgers. Mr Overton and Mr Henbosch are on the first floor, Fain shares the second floor with Mrs Simons and Rosie Flack is up in the attic. Where does that leave Mina?

Not here on the first floor, that's for sure. The seaward back and landward front are empty. She checks them to make sure, but her memory of dusting the two rooms the day before yesterday stands clear in her mind. The dust was thick enough to induce a slight feeling of shame. Clearly she's let some things slide in recent weeks.

The second floor, then? Obviously she should know beyond a shadow of a doubt, but brains are funny things and sometimes adrift in the sluggish tides of the night they can lose their bearings.

Fain ascends on tip-toe, finely balanced between sheepishness and unease. This is such an absurd thing to be happening! She knows every inch of this house. There isn't a room she hasn't played in, slept in, or (latterly) scrubbed and slaved and skivvied in.

So the emotion she feels most strongly, standing now at the end of a corridor she has never seen before, is naked terror.

There are no corridors at the Ocean View. The stairwell winds around a central space that's perfectly square, with the big domed skylight illuminating it from above. It has four storeys, with four rooms on every floor except the very top, where two slope-shouldered chambers crouch in the cramped space under the eaves.

The space where Fain is standing now can't possibly exist. It's not even in the same architectural style as the rest of the building. It's wide enough to be ostentatious, wasteful of space, and its ceiling is so high that she would not be able to touch it even with her extensible feather duster at full stretch. There are three doors on either side, all panelled in dark wood and all closed. The carpet has a design of brown flecks on a golden background. Two chandeliers hang down from that inaccessible ceiling on gilded chains. They're not lit, a fact for which she finds she's grateful. It may be frightening to stand here in the dark, but it would be so much worse to be picked out in a blaze of unrelenting light.

Fain wants very much to turn back, but she knows she can't. She's found her unwanted visitor at last, and it's not a person, it's a place—a place that has somehow attached itself to her house as a barnacle attaches itself to the pilings under a pier. She moves on stealthily, trying to make no sounds with her footfalls, staying close to the wall in case anyone might be watching, though she sees no sign of life.

She stops when she comes to the first pair of doors, reluctant to move on past them in case... well, in case there's someone or something in one of these unseen rooms that wishes her harm, and that might burst out upon her when she's moved on past it and irrevocably committed herself.

She opens the door on her own side of the corridor, just a crack, and peers inside. The room beyond is dark, but there's a light switch on the wall. Bracing herself for shock and flight, Fain turns on the light.

The room is a closet. Obviously it belongs to a woman, because a woman's clothes hang there. The dresses are so beautiful they take Fain's breath away. They're like the dresses from those long-ago parties, of which she still dreams sometimes. Above them, on shelves, hat-boxes sit in rows, their contents only to be guessed at. The names of semi-legendary shops in London and Paris adorn their outsides.

Hello? The voice is high and musical, like a tinkling of bells, and it's coming from behind her. Fain starts and turns around quickly. The door opposite her stands ajar, though she's sure it was closed a moment before.

Please help me, the voice says. *Nobody has been by here in so very long. Oh please don't leave me here! I beg you, save me. Save me before my cruel captor comes back to torture me again.*

"Who—who are you?" Fain asks. She speaks the words in a hoarse whisper, but evidently they carry.

My name hardly matters, the voice says sorrowfully. *I've all but forgotten it myself. I'm only a poor girl stolen from herself by a blackguard with a glittering eye and a pocketful of empty promises. Save me! Oh save me!*

Fain crosses the corridor. There's no need to turn on a switch this time, the room is already flooded with brightness. When she pushes the door fully open and enters she finds herself in a dining room. There is a long table at which a dozen chairs are set. Tall windows look out on a garden which—despite the fact that this is the middle of the night—is enjoying the brilliant sunshine of a Summer day.

On the wall facing Fain is a Doré woodcut of Lucifer, king of Hell, half-entombed in ice. His chin rests on his two fists, elbows down on the frozen plain. His expression reminds Fain of a sullen child who'd rather be out playing.

Apart from Lucifer, who is two-dimensional and made of paper, there's nobody in the room.

I'm right here, the voice says. *Come! Come! Help me!*

"Where?" Fain asks. She realises even as she says it, but only because she's used to talking to her mother whose current residence is an urn full of her own body's ashes. There's a vase on the table, exquisitely shaped and gorgeously decorated. It has a curious shape, very wide and deep, with a handle to either side and a neck that flares outward to become a broad, flat rim. There are figures on the vase of men on horseback, women dancing, temples, rampant beasts. The colours are so vibrant, so alive, they seem to bleed out onto the surrounding air. Its high glaze refracts the light from the overhead bulb into sparring rainbows.

Yes! You see me. Now take me. Take me away from here before he comes. Oh please, please!

Fain reaches out a hand. But her eyesight blurs for a moment, and acting on some premonition she doesn't try to interrogate she freezes. When she blinks away the mote or whatever it was she finds that she was mistaken about where the vase sat on the table. She had thought it was near the back but it's actually dead centre. It's also not quite so tall as she thought. Instead of seizing it by its narrow neck she was about to put her hand on its rim, which has an edge as sharp as any knife.

Well? The vase says. *What are you waiting for? Pick me up.*

The moment stretches. And finally the little silvery voice laughs. *Almost had you*, it says. *Might I still persuade you? A single drop will set me free. Bleed for me and I'll grant your every wish.*

"That's hard to believe," Fain says bluntly.

It's a lie. A single drop would bind you to me. And being bound, I'd make you spill the rest into my open mouth.

"That's a no, then."

Thought so. Come back if you change your mind.

Fain gets out of the room as quickly as she can. She's alarmed to find that the door has closed behind her, and the doorknob seems to squirm in her grip, resisting her for several long seconds before it opens. She slams it behind her, shutting off a mocking chuckle from that thin, shrill voice. She is badly shaken and more than a little discouraged. She knows, in a general sense, what kind of being she has just encountered. She knows, therefore, that she can't hope to hold her own against whoever or whatever it was that bound it. She needs to leave before she's discovered and challenged.

But now she finds she's lost her way. The corridor is gone, replaced by a circular arcade from which four separate hallways lead off at right angles to each other. None of them even remotely resembles the way she came.

She stands nonplussed at the centre of the circle, turning her head this way and that. No clues present themselves. No one way looks better than another. Beginning to panic now, Fain takes one at random, her gaze flicking to left and right as she walks in search of anything that looks like her own house. But there's nothing. She takes a left turn, a right. She breaks into a run. She knows she's most likely running deeper into the maze, but she can't control her own legs. She can barely keep from crying out for help.

She comes to another open atrium, this one with six ways leading from it. A sob escapes her. Again she runs at random. This time the corridor ends after a hundred steps in a blank, bare wall. She retraces her steps, but the atrium is gone. In its place is a cloister walk built around an open courtyard. This time the sky overhead is dark, as it should be, but three moons hang there. From the well in the centre of the courtyard comes a hollow, tortured moaning.

Fain runs on. A ballroom. A billiard room. A library whose shelves stretch higher than she can see. This place, this parasite house with its jaws locked on her own, is as big as a palace. It's mocking her with its endless extent.

Suddenly, though, as she steps out of the library into another hallway, she notices something on the floor at her feet. All this time, whenever she walked (or ran) on carpet it has borne the same design of small brown flecks on a golden background—the design she saw in that first hallway. But here it's different. Here it's plain gold except for the centre, between Fain's feet, where there is a pattern of intertwined snakes. They make a line that runs straight towards a specific doorway—one of very many. Beside the snakes woven right into the carpet's thick, luxurious pile, are cursive letters. *Fain*, they say, and then *follow*. All the snakes, Fain realises, are facing the same way.

She runs again, but this time only where the snakes tell her to. It could be a trap—most likely it is—but it's the only choice that presents beyond blindly blundering on with no hope of finding an exit. Ahead of her, wherever the way is dark, the lights go on so she can see the design and stay on the right path.

At last she stumbles through an arch, across a tiled and echoing space that looks as though it might be the choir of a church, and down a flight of stairs into a place she suddenly recognises as her own, her own house. Although she's descending she's at the very top of the building, stepping down into the attic space between Rosie's door and the empty room across from it.

She braces herself, turns and looks behind her. There's only a blank wall. The steps she just descended are gone.

Fain returns to her own room on legs that barely carry her. She feels she has had a very narrow escape, and it doesn't help at all that she doesn't know what she escaped from.

And where was Mina in all this? Where is she now? The mystery of where she sleeps is folded into the bigger mystery of why nobody—not even Fain herself—has even asked until now. Fain is Ocean View's manager and live-in landlord. She is the one who allocates rooms. It makes no sense at all that she misplaced a boarder in this careless, casual way.

So many things, now she thinks about it, make no sense. She hopes that when she goes back to her own room she will find Mina waiting for her there so they can have this out right now and get to the bottom of it. But the room is empty. It will have to wait until morning.

And by morning it's already too late.

※

There's a ringing in Fain's ears when she wakes. At first she thinks it's part of her dreams, in which doors and doorways, entrances and exits have figured very largely.

Then the front doorbell sounds again and she realises that the ringing was what woke her. She glances at the clock. It's late. She's missed breakfast, a thing that has never happened before. The boarders, especially Rosie and Mr Henbosch whose working days start and finish at precisely determined times, would have had to make shift for themselves.

Full of shame, she throws on last night's clothes and stumbles down the stairs to the front door. She's as quick as she can be, considering, but the bell sounds three more times before she reaches the door. The last ring is accompanied by the hammering of the caller's fist against the door, hard enough to make it shake in its frame.

Fain throws the door open, ready to give this peremptory whoever-it-is a piece of her mind, but she is thrown out when she sees him. He stands more than a head taller than her and somehow seems taller still, as if the body she can see is a down-payment on a larger body that will be delivered as and when her eyes and mind can process it. His bald head is adorned with strange markings, his dark eyes all pupil so they seem like black windows in a wall of pale yellow brick. Everything about him is hard and angular. The edges of his suit at shoulder and elbow look sharp enough to cut. The fabric itself is not just black but the super-black in which some deep-sea fish cloak themselves in order to rest unseen on the ocean's bottom. There are no folds or textures visible within it. It swallows light the way a sponge swallows water.

He places his hand on his chest with the fingers splayed and gives a very slight bow. "Good day to you," he says civilly. "I deeply regret any inconvenience this may cause, but I'm here to carry out an inspection of these premises. Are you the owner, or one of the tenants?" His voice is surprisingly thin, but it feels to Fain like a thinness that might be good for carving with.

"I'm the owner," Fain says. "And what do you mean by an inspection? Inspecting what? For whom? Who are you?" She folds her arms, openly belligerent. The fact that she's somewhat intimidated by this man makes her all the more determined to stand her ground.

The man regards her coldly for the space of a breath. For all the urbane polish of his manners and his opening sally he looks as though he's holding in with difficulty some very intemperate response. "Well now," he says, "I'm not obliged to explain those things to you. Let me show you this." He takes a folded sheet of paper from his pocket, opens it up and holds it unnecessarily close to her face. "As you see," he tells her, "this is a special license from the Home Office. It gives me right of entry to any house or commercial building in the town."

"The Home Office?" Fain stares at the document blankly. It does seem to confer the permissions her strange visitor has just mentioned. It also gives him a name: Ortho Aballach.

"Specifically," Ortho Aballach says, "the branch of the Home Office that deals with paranormal matters. But there's no need for me to waste any more of your time. Why don't you return to your chores while I carry out the tests and examinations that are required."

In the space of a moment, and without Fain having moved, the man is no longer standing in front of her but is past her, inside the house. Fain turns quickly, startled, to find him walking down the short hallway to the stairwell. He stands there very still with his eyes closed, as if listening.

"Excuse me—" Fain says, but he holds up his hand imperiously. After a moment he sweeps on up the stairs. Fain follows, at a run. "I didn't say you could come in!" she shouts after him.

On the first floor landing the man makes a full circuit, running his hands along the walls, before coming back to a place between the linen closet and the door to the landward back room which is 2B (or not 2B, Mr Henbosch has been known to append). By this time Fain has caught up with him and she gives his turned back a piece of her mind. "That paper, Mr…Aballach?" she says, "…may give you a right of access but it doesn't free you to go wherever you like without any explanation. This is still my house. Tell me what you're intending to do in it!"

The man doesn't even turn to face her, ignores her absolutely. "Ah," he says. "Yes. Oh yes. I think so." He places both hands against the plaster, fingers spread wide, and cocks his head to one side. His body is rigid, his expression one of intense concentration.

"I'm going to call the police," Fain says. "If you won't talk to me you can talk to them."

"Was there a door here recently?" Aballach—assuming that's his real name—demands. "You would certainly have noticed it. Most likely it would have been of varnished wood, standing out from the rest of this place by virtue of the quality of both wood and workmanship." He turns to stare at her, those black eyes shining and preternaturally wide.

Fain doesn't even respond to the implied insult. The reference to a door where no door should be is all she hears. *Don't tell him!* Her mother's voice sounds in her mind's ear, bolstering her own instinctive mistrust of this man. "I didn't see a door here," she says. Aballach searches her face, but she's told the literal truth and she holds his gaze.

The door to Mr Overton's room opens, providing a welcome distraction. Mr Overton peers out, presumably having heard the doorbell and the voices. "Miss Cabordet," he says. "We missed you at breakfast."

"I'm very sorry about that, Mr Overton," Fain answers. "I missed my alarm and slept too late."

He shakes his head. "It was fine. We helped ourselves, which I trust was acceptable." He looks from her to Aballach, then back again. "Is there a problem?"

"No." Fain thinks there very probably is, but she doesn't want to involve her boarders in it. "Really. Everything is fine." Mr Overton retreats.

Aballach sweeps on up the stairs. This time Fain doesn't scurry after him at once, but makes a side-trip to her room to retrieve her knife. Enough is enough. *Be careful, Jo!* Cass exhorts her. *He stinks of magic. I think he's dangerous.*

"I'm sure he is," Fain agrees. "But so am I."

When she comes out again she finds both the first and second floor landings empty. Aballach has ventured all the way up to the loft space where Rosie's room is. Once again he has gone without hesitation to a blank stretch of wall that looks no different to the rest. When Fain comes up to join him he has his cheek pressed to it. His right arm too, at full stretch and with the palm inwards as if he's trying to engage the wall in a slow dance.

"What about here?" he demands. "Did you see a door in this space? Or if not a door, an archway? An opening? Or any physical space that didn't belong?"

"No," Fain says—again, truthfully. This was where she touched down, as it were, after her sojourn in that other house, but when she turned back the breach had sealed and there was nothing to see.

The man drops down on all fours. His dark eyes scan the carpet, and at the same time he probes it with the tips of his fingers. "Here, I think," he mutters. "Something. Something that has a little of her feel to it. Again, I must ask you—"

He glances up at this point and sees what Fain is holding in her hand. "Ah," he concludes. He climbs very slowly to his feet.

Fain isn't holding the knife *en garde*, as if she intended to thrust or swipe with it. She has no experience of that kind of fighting at all and she suspects the man's much longer reach would make any such attack moot. She's holding it by the tip, her arm tilted back with the hand just below waist height. At this range she knows she can make the throw with ease. The man is such a big target there's no possibility of missing.

He doesn't seem alarmed at the prospect though. He only looks at the knife, then at Fain's face, and eventually shrugs.

"Where is she?" the man asks, ignoring all of this. "I don't intend harm to anyone else, but I will take her. And I'll deal summarily with anyone who stands in my way."

"Oh my lord!" Fain says. "I've never been dealt with summarily before. I'm almost curious. But I'll deal summarily with your windpipe if you try it. Now get out of my house."

The man quirks an eyebrow, his contempt for Fain understated and yet absolutely blatant. He flexes his fingers.

"You heard Miss Cabordet." It's Mr Overton. This time he has emerged fully from his room and come halfway up the stairs. He is gripping a poker in his hand, and his expression is resolute, bordering on stern. Mrs Simons has come out too, and like Mr Overton she's armed, although only with an ornamental paperweight in the shape of the Eiffel Tower.

Aballach doesn't so much as glance at either of them. "I assume you know what she is," he says to Fain.

"I have no idea who you're talking about."

He's readying a spell, Cass interjects. *Watch his right hand.*

Fain has already seen the tell-tale twitching of Aballach's fingers, but there's very little she can do about it. Outside of a little foretelling now and again she has no magic. Her mother's gift did not come down to her.

"You're lying," the man says. "She's been here. And that almost certainly means she's here still. It takes her some little while to gather herself and move. I did mention, did I not, that I'm here with official approval and authority? I'm a binder of demons. And though Hove Harbour has traditionally seen fit to exclude those who ply my trade, in this case they don't have any choice. My writ comes from Whitehall itself. A dangerous demon is loose and I'm licensed to use any means necessary to find and constrain her."

"All that's as may be," Fain says, "but it won't be an easy thing to do with a perforated lung. If I were you, I'd think about plying my trade somewhere else. And I'd do it summarily."

Aballach considers for a moment or two with a solemn frown on his face. Then slowly, as though through the exertion of some great effort of self-control, he smiles. "Dear lady," he says, "I believe our acquaintance may have started out on the wrong foot. I've barely been under your roof for two minutes and already we're exchanging threats and insults, like fishwives at market. That's not how civilised people proceed, and for my part in it I humbly apologise."

"That's a start." Fain lowers the knife, but she doesn't take her eyes off the man and she doesn't unbend enough to return that frankly unconvincing smile. Mr Overton and Mrs Simons also stand down, though they pointedly do not return to their rooms. They mean to see this out. "But if you're really sorry," Fain goes on, "then the best thing you can do is to take yourself off and not come back here. We're not harbouring your demon." Or are they? It suddenly occurs to her to wonder, but certainly not to confess or explain.

"Did I mention the reward?" Aballach asks blandly.

"No, you did not. What reward?"

"Fifty…" He taps his chin. "No, a hundred thousand pounds. For information leading to, et cetera. Give me the one I came for, or put me on the right track to find her, and I'll pay you on this very spot."

"You must have very deep pockets," Mr Overton observes drily.

"No," Aballach says. "But I have magic. It comes to the same thing."

"Fairy gold's worthless."

"Coin of the realm, I assure you. I'd use magic to fetch it, not to make it. I'm a very rich man." Aballach's black eyes seem to expand, becoming a black mirror in which Fain sees herself. A hundred images flicker before her gaze. The skylines of foreign cities, canyons and mountains whose names she knows only from books, parties, parades and masquerade balls, dining on meat and sleeping in velvet.

She opens her mouth to offer up some more defiance, but the words fail her.

"I'll leave you my card," Aballach says.

He arches an eyebrow, clicks his tongue. Seven digits are inscribed in fire on the wall behind his head.

Fain scans them, letting nothing show on her face. "There's no area code."

"Where I live there is no area as such. There's only me. My phone number is the visible expression of a modest cantrip. You don't even need a phone, really. Say the numbers out loud, and then my name. I'll come. Or don't, and I'll come anyway. But in that case I'll come in flame and fury and despite."

He rises into the air and drifts out into the stairwell. Nothing propels him apart from small, understated movements of his hands. He turns, hanging there, to regard Mr Overton's poker. In the blink of an eye it becomes a snake: a cobra, with its hood extended to the full, rears up and makes to bite him. Mr Overton drops it with a yelp of alarm, and when it hits the floor it's just a poker again.

"You need to make a choice." Aballach's tone is soft, but the smile is gone and the grimness has returned to take its place. Though he's bobbing in the air like a child's balloon he's truly terrifying. He addresses himself only to Fain—just as the bribe he offered was for her alone. And now that she ponders on this she believes she knows why.

"Possibly," he tells her, "you feel your pride is bound up in this, or your integrity. Your humanity, even. That it's wrong to give someone you know, someone for whom you perhaps feel some affection, into a stranger's power. But—to repeat myself—this is a demon. However she presents herself, she's of a race whose writ is long ended and she has no rights of any kind in this kingdom. The law doesn't protect her and the civil authorities have washed their hands of her. Furthermore, and this is the point I'd stress most heavily, she belongs to me. If you stand between me and my rightful property, there will most certainly be consequences—not just for you but for everyone under this roof.

"Think better, and call me. A single word—let's say, the word *yes*—will be enough. I'll extract no apologies or penances. I'll pay you the price I offered, and wait while you count it.

"But Miss Cabordet, I won't wait long. If you choose not to give Esuluminax over to me, I'll return when she's in her other guise and unable to hide. I'll tear her loose from the fabric of this house where she's attached herself, and I won't do it gently. The house is unlikely to survive. And the rest of you will have to make shift as best you can."

He makes a negligent gesture with his left hand. The skylight shatters, showering shards of glass down into the stairwell. Somehow none of it touches Aballach himself. He points with his right index finger. The banister rail in front of Fain explodes into splinters. The invisible force that broke it doesn't quite manage to stop before it reaches her too. It lifts her off her feet and throws her backward.

There is a moment, or perhaps several moments, when she's not entirely certain what's happening. Her ears are ringing, and there is an iron taste in her mouth where she has bitten her tongue.

"Take it slowly, Miss Cabordet," Mr Overton beseeches her. "You've had quite a shock." He's at her side, and she's lying full length on the ground. Some time must have passed, but whether it's seconds, minutes or hours she has no idea. She tries to sit up, manages it on the second attempt. Mrs Simons is there too, and so is Mina. It's not clear where she's come from. For a moment she's stark naked. Then she seems to remember herself and instantly she's fully dressed in sweater, jeans and black plimsolls.

She kneels before Fain and clasps her hand. "Are you all right?" she asks urgently, her voice full of alarm and concern. "Fain, did he hurt you?"

"Where did you spring from?" Fain asks weakly. "You weren't here a moment ago."

"I hid when he came. I'm so sorry. I brought this on you, and I'm sorry. I didn't think he'd find me so quickly."

Fain gives her a stare that's wary, closed. "You owe me more than an apology, Mina," she says. "You owe me—and all of us—an explanation."

Mina's eyes narrow, as if she's readying a barbed reply. But after a moment's silence she nods. "You're right," she says, putting on her old meekness again. "I do. You see, I lied to you when I first—"

"Not now." Fain climbs to her feet, flicking wood splinters from her arms and chest. "I said *all* of us. This evening, when everyone is back, you'll tell us the whole story."

They have their conference in the kitchen, the only space in the house that offers enough room and enough chairs for them all. Cass is present too, her urn having been relocated from the bedroom mantel to the centre of the kitchen table for the duration. While Mr Henbosch and Mr Overton (with more noise and bustle than is strictly necessary) boil up a pot of tea and liberate some Fox's Assorted biscuits from Fain's private stash, Mina begins her story. She speaks tentatively at first, picking her words with some care, but her voice soon gains in confidence and takes on a more emphatic tone. The scenes she is describing sometimes escape from her mind and roil in the air above her head, to the alarm of some of the party and the admiration of others.

"First of all," Mina says, "I should confess that my name is not Mina Sellicks. It's Esuluminax. I'm of the Brithual Sistren, the daughters of Lilith's daughters."

"Demons," says Mrs Simons.

"Demons, yes." Mina nods demurely. "I would have said that straight out but I know how you of Eve and Adam's line hate us."

"Because you used to steal our children."

Mina looks pained. "Where did you hear that?" she asks. "Did you read it in a tabloid newspaper? You might also have read that we tempt priests into sin and then drag them down to Hell, and that we wear the entrails of babies as hats."

"Are you saying you don't do those things?" Mr Overton demands.

Mina shakes her head. "No. None of them. It's propaganda. The binders need some colour for what they do, and so they spread lurid stories about us. Entrails would make a terrible hat, and priests sin all the time without any encouragement from us. There's nothing to be gained."

"You *did* try to tempt us though," Rosie points out.

"I tried to please you," Mina says. "I do that in all sorts of ways, as you must surely have noticed. And there's a reason for it, which I'll explain to you. But none of my kind has ever preyed on you. Our biggest sin is pride, not hate or greed." Mina sighs, shakes her head. "We had no real conception, in the dawn times, of what you truly were. The span of your existence was so short, and your understanding so slight. We thought of you as clever animals. We felt no kinship, no obligation. Do you feel any for the animals that grace your table?"

"You'll make yourself no friends with words like that," Rosie points out quietly.

"I'm only speaking the truth." Mina's gaze sweeps them all, defiant, but then she bows her head and looks at the table. Her fingertip traces the curved line left there by the bottom of a teacup. "And I'm not defending the way we thought, the way we behaved. I'm only remembering. We were arrogant. We knew the world when angels still walked in it, and we looked down on them every bit as much as we did on you. The pigeons, we called them. When they strode by we called *rou-cou, rou-cou*."

She describes with passion she doesn't try to hide a world that was very simple and painted in the brightest of colours. Demon-kin danced and played all across the universe, and in other places that were bigger still. They lived under the interdict of God, but God had always kept to himself a great deal and if they didn't bother him then he seemed for the most part to forget they were even there.

"We just got used to thinking of ourselves as having the keys to Creation. Being in charge of everything. We forgot there was any writ but ours. And in a way, you know, we were everything we thought we were. It was only that we couldn't become anything more. That was our downfall. Being immortal means you never change. The one generation of us is all there will ever be. Whereas your kind—and I mean no disrespect—change is the very thing you're made of. Growing like wheat, falling like wheat, building and breaking all the time. Your seasons are less than the blink of an eye to us. And every time we blink, you're different again."

She gathers herself, coming to the point of her recital. "There is a man, a user of magic. His name is Ortho Aballach. He's the man some of you met today. The man who came into Fain's house in search of me, only she spat defiance at him and wouldn't give me over."

"He seemed to think I could," Fain said. "That my word, my saying yes, would make his work easier."

"It would." Mina is emphatic, even urgent. "This is your siege, Fain, the seat of your power."

Fain winces a little. "What power?"

"More than you know. The places we love are the places where we're strongest. He sees where I'm anchored. But let me explain Aballach before I come to the rest of it.

"I think, by the way you measure time, he counts as old. He's lived a great deal longer than a single century, anyway. He's always been his own laboratory, using his magic to repair and improve his own body, to make himself as much like us as he can. I think envy of what others have is a large part of what drives him, and when it comes to the Sistren he envies us that we're of the frame eternal.

"Some while ago, having refined and extended his own powers and built himself up into something truly formidable, he bought a binder's license from the government and set himself to hunt down one of my sisters. Her name was Achlys Mist of Sorrow. She knew she was being tracked, and didn't mind at all. The novelty of it amused her, and she felt herself more than a match for whatever it was that was sniffing her spoor. She led him a fine dance, across all the realms and reaches. But he caught up with her at last.

"He fought her, and he won. And having won he exulted over her. He could have killed her—he was breaker as well as binder, had the right to kill endorsed by license—but he changed her instead, locking her into one shape where my kind are used to taking whatsoever form we please. Being fond of antiquities and of alcohol he made her into a *krater*, the vessel in which the ancient Greeks mixed wine and water for a feast."

Rosie shudders. "That's a monstrous thing to have done, if it really happened."

"I think I met your sister last night," Fain says. "She spoke to me. Tried to—to wound me, I think. Or make me wound myself."

"How?" Mr Overton asks, bewildered and clearly frightened by all this talk of monsters and magic. "How did you meet her? Where?"

"Here." Mina puts a finger between her breasts, taps her sternum. "You've been there too, Mr Overton, and you, Rosie. But you have to let me speak, or you won't understand.

"Aballach was very pleased with himself, having subdued one of my deathless kind. He was also very excited to discover that doing so had increased his store of power. He'd only thought to put Achlys in shackles, but once she was there he found that he himself was on the other end of the same chain. He could draw on my sister's might to augment his own, and she couldn't choose but give it."

So he hunted again, Cass says. Mr Overton, who of all the boarders has the least to do with his landlady's dead mother, starts a little and looks over his shoulder.

"Oh yes. He hunted many times. And he didn't always have it his own way. We're a fierce breed. Often when he went for one of us he came away bloodied. Some of those wounds won't heal, he can only mitigate the pain and the damage with his magic. But he didn't stop. I don't think he knew how to. And whenever he bested any one of us he changed us. My sister Kasadya he made into a painting of herself, rendered in an angular modernist style. My beloved Lethoziminiar is now a pear tree in his garden from which he plucks a fruit whenever he passes."

"And you," Fain says. "You were one of those he hunted."

"No." Mina's voice is hard. "I hunted him. I wanted to put a stop to his depredations. I knew the risk I was taking, but I thought I was strong enough to beat him. I had armour that an angel had worn, and one of the Furies' scorpion whips. I didn't think I could possibly fail. But I did, obviously. Aballach deployed my sisters' strength against me. He was too much for me. I fell before his attack. And then he made me into his house."

"His house?" Mr Henbosch echoes. He looks perturbed.

"I mean it quite literally." Mina darts a look at Fain. It seems this is something she very much wants her to understand. "It was the most ambitious of all his many makings. The sistren aren't made of flesh and blood. They're not fixed in any one shape, or any one substance, so changing me wasn't the hard part. Fixing me in that changed shape was another matter. He drew on all the power he had, both his own native magic and what he'd stolen from my kindred. He forced me to become…well, what I said. A house. A dwelling. A thing made up of rooms, of walls and ceilings, rather than limbs and organs, skin and bone.

"He gave himself up to his ambition, and his self-love. At that time he was living in a small end-terrace house in Kensington—pleasant enough, and in a fashionable neighbourhood, but he wanted more. A mansion. A palace. An alcazar greater than anything that had been in the world before.

"So he decided not to put it in the world at all. He built it in a different space entirely, a small reality he made for himself, that answers to his every whim. And he made me, likewise, to be responsive to all his needs. If he wanted to walk, I grew a cloister for him. If he had a yen for a fine cigar, I made a smoking room. If he wanted to read, a library. I was as big or as small as he needed me to be at any given time. Mostly I was vast, because Aballach's tastes aren't what you would call modest. I grew halls and wings and annexes bigger than cathedrals."

Mina pauses and looks up. "This is why I showed you the stamp albums, Mr Overton—and Rosie, why I offered you cake. I wasn't trying to lure you in and trap you or hurt you. I just read your desires and tried to satisfy them. I couldn't help myself. Aballach's magic forced me."

"I'm sorry I didn't try the cake, then," Rosie says, with a wry laugh. "I imagine it would have been good."

"It would have been the best thing you ever tasted."

"Damn."

"Wait, though," Fain says, "that explains how you came to be a house, Mina. It doesn't explain how you came to be rooms in *my* house."

"Which is also how I came to lose my leg." Mina glances down at her prosthetic limb, which seems in that moment to glow with an inner light. "I told you it was a choice, Fain. But I didn't tell you what I was choosing between.

"I lived under Aballach, and he lived in me, for a very long time. Years. Decades. It's not easy for me to explain what that was like. I felt...infested. Contaminated. There was a canker in me, a gall, and the gall had made itself my master. Every day was torment. I was a prisoner, but where most prisoners are thrown into a cell already made, I was made to become the cell in which I was confined.

"I was also forced to witness the way he lived. It was no accident or aberration that he only pursued those of my kin who manifested in female form. He hates women and treats them abominably. I watched them come and go in their dozens, entranced at first by Aballach's largesse and flattering attentions, then distressed by his growing indifference after he lost interest in them, and finally chased away by his cruelties, which progressed quickly from the petty to the purely tyrannical.

"I tried many times to escape. I would wait until Aballach left and exert all my strength, hauling on what I imagined were the chains that bound me. The effort *hurt*, so I thought it must be achieving something. But I was never able to get free. And at last I realised that this was because I was pulling against a part of my own self. The pocket universe in which Aballach had built wasn't a thing that was separate from me, it was a part of me. He had made it, just as he had made the house, out of my body. I couldn't get free of that place without leaving a part of myself behind."

"Is that what you did?" Fain asks. She can't forebear from covering Mina's hand, which is resting on the table, with her own. Whether they can be lovers again after all the lies and misdirections is a question that can't even be asked right now—or possibly ever—but it hurts her to see so much pain in Mina's eyes.

"In the end," she says, "yes. When I'd borne all I could. And when I saw that there was no other way. I tore myself loose. Like a fox chewing off its own leg to get out of a trap, I suppose. I was greatly reduced. Less than a shadow of myself. For so long I'd thought of myself as greater than you sons of Adam and daughters of Eve, but now… now I was brought so low I could only think of myself as an animal in a snare."

"I'd heard," Mrs Simons says carefully, "that your kind are like lizards or starfish. I mean, when it comes to severed limbs. That the loss of an arm, a leg, even a head doesn't trouble you overmuch."

If Mina is offended by the comparison she doesn't show it. "That's most often true," she agrees. "As I said, we're not made of flesh and blood. We weave our bodies out of our own will. But it was my will that Aballach had bound, Mrs Simons. An inmost part of me, not an accidental one.

"So when I broke myself in two I felt the agony of it. The loss, like a hole in the heart of me. I almost died from pain, from shock, from grieving. The ache didn't subside, either. I kept feeling the part of me that was missing, and it felt as though it was on fire. I did what I could to heal myself. I went to sleep for a long time, which is a thing the sistren do after we've taken serious hurt. But I woke up no different—and though I tried on many shapes and guises I found I couldn't knit myself whole again.

"Whatever piece of my being I left behind me when I broke free, it was clear that I would bear the mark of it from then onward in any shape I wore. If I'm a woman, I'm a woman as you see me now with just the one leg rather than the two the rest of you have. If I'm a dwelling place, I'm only rooms in a house and not the whole of it."

"My house is made of rooms," Fain says gently. "And each room in it has been a home to someone. There's no shame in that."

"No shame perhaps, but no peace either." For the first time Mina's voice thickens and her eyes well with tears. Fain would have sworn if anyone had asked her that demons were incapable of crying. "I find...just as I left a little of my own self behind, I took some of the binding, of Aballach's interdiction with me. I can't go a whole day without at some point shedding this body and putting on the shape of a house. Parts of a house, I should say. Rooms and hallways and courtyards and corridors. I'm like those men that are wolves with their fur on the inside of their skins, who turn the right side out again when the moonlight touches them. Only in my case it's not wolf I turn but architecture.

"And now Aballach has found me. He was never going to stop looking— not when I took so many of his treasures away with me in my rooms. And he means what he says. If you stand in his way he'll strike you down, with as little care as he showed me. Less, perhaps, because he's got nothing to gain from any of you. You've no choice but to do as he says—to call those numbers out, say the word and let him take me."

And now the tear falls. Only the one, though, full and fat and catching the light from the ceiling bulb, making its way down the centre of her cheek as straight as if its route had been plotted with plumb and line.

Ooh, I never saw such pretty crying, Cass exclaims—not to the room at large but whispering in her daughter's ear. *Not in real life, anyway. Only in a movie house.*

Fain sees the artifice too, but she finds it makes no difference. Everyone has their own way of asking for help, and Mina has been frank about the pride and hauteur of her kind. She won't beg. Not in words, at least.

"Well," Fain says, "we'll have to see about that. But I've more questions yet, Mina, if you don't mind."

Mina nods, tilting her head a little so that everyone gets the full benefit of the tear.

"All those times when we sat around the table and the spirits wouldn't speak to us, was that your doing?"

"Yes."

"You had the power to charm them silent?"

"It's not hard. Ghosts are small, frail things. It's harder to make them speak up in the first place than it is to shut them down."

Cheeky madam! Cass exclaims.

"And the memories we had of you coming here to Ocean View. Those were all false, so where did they come from? Was that you too?"

"It was. I was trying to hide, and I knew that if I just came and knocked on the door in the normal way of things, you'd have questions. I thought it would be better if I'd been here a long while, so you all took me for granted. I'm sorry to have lied to you all."

"It was a little more than a lie though," Fain persists. "You reached inside our heads and planted ideas there. Moved the furniture around."

You did that to *me*, is the unspoken part of that speech. You were never naked when you lay in my arms. You wore those lies every night and every day.

But there's a second unspoken meaning too, and Mina jumps on that one to avoid tangling with the first. "That's so, Fain, and it's a power I can wield, but it wouldn't work on Aballach. I tried more than once after he first took me, but his mind is proof against enchantments. He's very sensitive to magic of any kind. Sees it even when it's not being used but only lying quiet. That's how he found out that I was here. And it's how he hunts us. The children of Lilith's children are soaked through with magic. In his eyes we're like beacons that can be seen a great way off."

Fain sits back, palms pressed against the wood of the table. It's part of the house and therefore, in a way, it's part of her. Curious that she should only feel this way now, when she's met someone for whom that connection is not a metaphor but a literal fact—and a burden, not a source of strength. Still, someone has come against her in the place where she lives and where others' lives are entwined with hers. That's not acceptable, and she doesn't intend to let it pass.

"I suppose," she says, "he can take care of himself in a fight."

"You saw for yourself. He has so many spells at his beck, he never wants for an answer when anyone comes at him. I'd dearly love to fight him again and cast him down, but I'm much diminished from what I was. The years of being a slave have weakened and lessened me in more ways than I can say. And even when I was at my strongest Aballach was too much for me. There's nothing that can threaten him except for a mage that's stronger than himself. And as I said, you couldn't hope to surprise him. He knows where other magics are, in any space where he goes—and how strong they are, and of what kind."

"Well then." Fain stands. "It seems I've a lot to do and not much time to do it in. Aballach said he'd come back tonight. I'd imagine he means after midnight but I can't rely on that."

"You're going to help me?" Mina asks. For all the theatrical overemphasis of that tear she sounds genuinely surprised and relieved.

"I'll do what I can," Fain says.

"What about the rest of us?" Mr Henbosch asks.

"That's for you to decide, Mr Henbosch. As landlady I feel I have to intervene when my boarders are threatened. You'll all have to choose for yourselves." The truth is that Fain doesn't even know yet what she herself is going to do. She has the smallest germ or seed from which a plan might grow, but it's not much and she knows they don't have a great deal of time.

"I'd like to help too," Rosie says. "Any man that forces a woman into the wrong shape is a bastard in my book and needs taking down a peg. If there's anything I can do to fox this gombeen, count me in the party."

"Let me throw my name in too," Mr Overton says, with more asperity in his voice than Fain has ever heard there. "Mr Aballach is a bully, and bullies need to be dissuaded. Also, if I'm honest, the fellow made a fool of me today and it rankles. I'd relish the chance to pay him out."

"If anyone's to be made a fool of," offers Mr Henbosch, "you should consult with an expert. Fooling is what I'm best at."

Mrs Simons makes a sour face. "I'm still angry with you, Mina Sellicks, for interfering with my divinations like that. You made me think I was losing my mind—and my knack, which is worse. But I'll not stand out when all my friends are fighting. If you can use me, Fain, you can have me. I'd only ask in return that Mina apologise to my spirits when we're done for clapping her hand over their mouths like that."

"Willingly," Mina says. "Thank you, Mrs Simons. Thank you all. I swear never to be careless or contemptuous of humankind ever again." She looks at Fain when she says this, almost shyly. "I think of them—of you—very differently now. And of myself too."

Fain glances at the urn. "What about you, Mum?"

Oh, who cares what I think?

"I do. Otherwise I wouldn't ask, would I?"

Well then, I think this young lady—although she's neither of those things, truth be told—took advantage of us. I think it's none of our business helping her out of a mess she helped her own self into in the first place. If I heard her right, she said it was her that went looking for this Aballach, not the other way around. If that's so then by rights it ought to rest between the two of them to sort this out.

"Except that Aballach broke our skylight," Fain points out. "Threatened us. Said he'd huff and puff and knock our house down."

I know, and I'm not done yet. Mina, you brought this down on yourself and then you went and brought it down on us too. You should be ashamed to hide behind us now. But these binders and breakers are no more nor less than thugs. Thugs with a piece of paper saying their thuggery is official and above board. So all in all, I say we should teach Ortho Aballach a lesson he won't forget in a hurry."

"Then we're agreed," Fain says. "Mrs Simons, now the bones are free to talk again, would you mind asking them when Aballach will come back? It would be useful to know how long we've got."

"Of course." Mrs Simons gets to her feet at once and makes for the door—then comes back and downs the last swig of her tea. She takes the last two custard creams from the Fox's Assorted with her too. "Waste, want, what not," she says cheerfully.

Fain gets up too. "Perhaps the rest of you should take some rest," she says. "It's like to be a long, wild night. Mother, if you wouldn't mind, go with Mrs S and help her with the divination. I'd like a word with Mina alone."

Cass raises no objection to this. Mrs Simons takes up the urn and leaves, followed by Rosie and the two gentlemen. Fain and Mina are left alone. Mina looks into Fain's eyes, then her courage seems to falter and she stares at the floor for a while. Fain waits this out until finally Mina meets her gaze again.

"That was quite a story," Fain says.

"Every word of it was true."

"I know it was. I'm no seer like Mrs Simons, but the truth has a ring for me. I usually know it when I hear it. Then again, Mina, you bundled a great many lies past me when you came, so perhaps I'm only taking one more false coin out of the same purse."

"You're not," Mina says. "I swear it, Fain, I'll never lie to you again."

"Well never is a long time. But I'd like a straight answer on one thing, if it's not too much to ask."

"Anything!"

"You said the gifts you gave us came from the effect of Aballach's magic on you—forcing you to respond to other people's needs and desires."

"Yes. So?"

"So is that why you came to my bed?"

Mina's face goes through some changes at these words—showing pain at first, then bitterness, then nothing at all. "I can see why you'd think that," she says. "And I don't know how to answer you. Truly, I don't. I want to say that I came to you because of what I felt for you. For you, and for your house. That seeing you here, on this ground and under this roof, I wasn't sure where you ended and the house began. I thought... I thought I'd found another like myself, that was half and half. And it's not that, it's only how everyone here depends on you and how they come together around you. But still, I wasn't altogether wrong. In any case I believe I came to you because I wanted to be with you.

"But how can I say that?" Mina shrugs with clenched fists, a gesture that's eloquent of helpless rage. "How can I know, Fain? I'm well aware of what Aballach's magic makes me do, but I don't know how deeply it's sunk into me. I don't know how much of my heart is my own and how much his remaking and overwriting. I can't promise you what I'll choose, if a choice is ever given me. And I never loved a mortal before, woman or man, so all of this would be new and strange even if it weren't for—"

She gets no further. Fain goes to her and kisses her silent. A tension—a terror, even—that she'd struggled to admit to herself drains out of her. "We'll speak of it when you're free then," she says. "I'm glad you made no promises. Promises are too easy, for my kind as well as yours. And to tell you the honest truth, Mina, I wasn't sure of my own feelings until I thought I might lose you. Now I think... well, I think I want to find out at my leisure where we're going. And I've no intention of letting Aballach take you away from me before we're done."

They hold and reassure each other for some little while. "You were not tempted—even a little bit—by the reward?" Mina ventures in an interval between kisses.

"Oh, that." Fain tuts dismissively. "I've fantasised for years about leaving this place. About seeing the world. But I'd not take one bent farthing from a man that offers threats and bribes in the same breath. And in any case I find that my mood at the moment is very much for staying put."

More kisses follow these words. But time is short and all this sweetness feels like a luxury right now. Fain is the first to pull away.

"Would you be able to take your other shape now, Mina?" she asks. "I need to go inside you."

"Yes," Mina says. "Of course. It's holding this shape that's hard. I can be rooms whenever I want to. But what's inside me that you want?"

"Our last confederate," Fain says. "We're a force to be reckoned with as we are, but we're not quorate yet."

❧

This time when Fain enters the dining room she sees that it's blustery autumn in the garden outside, with red and orange leaves gusting in a wind from nowhere. The vase on the table, that she now knows is a *krater*, holds its silence.

"Give you good day, Achlys," Fain says. "Your sister Esuluminax said to say hello."

The vase still says nothing. Fain pulls back a chair and sits down. She takes her time, letting her eye wander over the designs on the vase, the many and varied scenes from an imagined antiquity. After a little while she extends her hand and flicks the vase with the back of a fingernail. It rings with a pure, sustained note.

Are you looking to vex me? the vase demands, with dangerous mildness.

"Not at all," Fain says. "I was only admiring you. That's a fine glaze you've got. And some lovely colours."

You're mocking me. I should warn you that's not a safe pastime.

Fain shakes her head. "I'm not mocking you, Achlys Mist of Sorrow. But honestly, it is a little sad to see you in this state. Esuluminax told me how great you were, back in the day. Masters of Creation, she said. Looking down on angels. Dancing and revelling in the sight of God, as if you were daring him to pick a fight with you. And now… Well, what's to be said? Ortho Aballach has taken a sad toll of you."

And of many more since. So?

"So, Esuluminax told me that the binder used your power when he went after your sisters. And theirs too, of course, once he had them, but you were the first and greatest and the foundation he built on."

True! All true! The chains he wrapped around me enforce my will as well as my body.

"Your body being mostly will to begin with, Esuluminax said. And I can see that. It's not as though a wine bowl is the truth of you, is it? The truth of you is something much bigger and stranger, that lives in change and scoffs at shape."

You're describing something you couldn't begin to understand. But all of that is true.

"Would you answer me a question, then? Because it's puzzling me. You said if I shed my blood on you I'd be bound to you and you could feed on me. Was that also true?"

Try, and learn.

"Not I, thank you very much."
Was that your question?
"No." Fain leaned forward. "My question is this."

※

They're all waiting when Fain comes back out through a door at the back of the kitchen that should lead nowhere but to the pantry.

"Well?" Mrs Simons demands.

"She's with us. How long have we got?"

"An hour and a half, the bones said. He'll come down through the broken skylight. I think he likes the dramatic effect."

"Good." Fain nods. "Thank you, Mrs S. Let's bolt the front door, then, and start to make ready. Mr Henbosch, Mr Overton, could you go and fetch the…" she's already forgotten the word "…the wine bowl thingummy. Mina will show you the way. Just follow the pattern on the carpet and it will take you straight there. Be very careful around Achlys. She wants to be free, but she also wants to feed. She'll try to trick you if she can, for all that she says she's on our side. Wear those heavy gloves and move slowly when you handle her. Be wary of any sharp edges."

"Don't worry about us," Mr Henbosch assures her. "Nobody tricks the trickster, Miss Cabordet." Mr Overton rolls his eyes and hefts the wheelbarrow from the back garden, which he's brought indoors for this expedition. He trundles it away and Mr Henbosch follows.

"Is there anything we can help with?" Rosie asks.

"Yes." Fain nods. "If you've got your equipment ready…"

"It's only hypodermics, a micro-filter and a pump. I got them from a friend at the A and E, no questions asked."

"Then as soon as Mina has stopped being a house and turned into a woman again, you can start drawing off her blood. Mrs Simons, if you wouldn't mind, check in with the bones again and see what else they can tell you about Aballach's past. Anything we can use in the decorations. Mum, are you with me?"

Of course I am, Cass all but snaps. *But you still haven't told me what you want me to do. I'm sitting here like a lemon.*

"Like the ghost of a lemon, you mean. You're not that, though. You're the most important part of the plan."

Am I then? Why are you buttering me up, Josephine Cabordet?

"I'm not. But I'm going to ask you to do something you said you never would."

Something I said…? Oh Jo, you can't mean…

"I do, though. I want you to open up the Star Dome."

※

It's a big ask, but Fain knows this. She's got her own rose-tinted glasses, after all, and her own reasons for looking back on those lost days with an aching fondness that's like a bereavement.

Hove Harbour had its fair share of cabarets and nightclubs back when Joseph and Cassandra Cabordet first moved there, but Joseph had ambitions that went beyond just getting a slot on someone else's bill.

"Are you sure you're up for this, Cass?" Joseph asked his wife. There was at least an appearance of concern in his voice, though he couldn't keep from showing his excitement too.

"Watch me," Cass said, and she meant it. She'd been saving up her power for months, weaving charms and cantrips into a tangled skein that she kept in the front of her mind, turning and turning. It was a magic on a scale she'd never tried before, but she'd found a way to make it be a hundred smaller magics tied together like knots in a string.

She stood in the stairwell of the run-down boarding house they'd just bought, facing the bare back wall. Three-year-old Fain peeped out from behind her, feeling the snap and fizz of spells in the air, the hairs on her arms and on the back of her neck standing up. She held on tight to a fold of Cass's skirt, as if the tide of enchantment that was about to be unleashed might wash her away.

"Room," Cass said. The word wasn't a spell, it was only a mnemonic for a spell already cast, a tug on the first knot in that string that loosed it and tugged on the next, and so on all the way down.

Magic exploded from her in a flood of unnameable colours. It splashed against the featureless wall, where suddenly there was a double door, the door thrown open, the space on the other side filled out, given texture and depth and volume by successive waves of arcane power. Cass laughed out loud. She couldn't help herself. She had spent her whole life weaving tiny charms, fear-nots and wake-wards and luck-bringers, and all the while she had saved the biggest part of herself for this. She had been an iceberg bobbing gently on an interior ocean, and only now did workaday reality, like a slow and stately ship, break open against the scope and majesty of her.

The Star Dome was a hundred strides from end to end. The walls were billowing smoke shot with waves of light that danced and pulsed as if it was alive. The ceiling was the night sky, but with the brilliance of the stars undimmed as they might show themselves to someone outside the curtain of atmosphere. The acoustics were perfect, with an uncanny intimacy as if wherever you were sitting the music was coming from directly in front of you.

It was a once-in-a-lifetime thing, she told Fain much later, when Fain was old enough to understand. The store of power in her replenished itself when she cast her charms, but it would not come back from this. She was spending herself in a single gesture, swapping her greatest gift for a dream—and not even her own dream but her husband's. It was Joseph who wanted to manage his own venue, and at first he did a reasonable job of it. The ineffable beauty of the Star Dome's décor sold itself, no matter who was in the night's line-up. Saturday nights were sold out weeks or months in advance.

In the longer term, Joseph's insistence on always putting himself at the top of the bill was a policy that led to diminishing returns. So too was the preferential treatment he gave to his own circle of friends, one of whom was the pestilential clarinettist with whom he romantically absconded when he'd steered the Star Dome into bankruptcy and couldn't face his wife and daughter across the breakfast table any more.

All that heartache, all that terrible waste and irreversible error, and now here was Fain asking Cass to set it all to one side for a little while and open the Dome for one last night, one final cabaret by special invitation only.

She wasn't surprised when her mother didn't answer straight away. She was anxious though. Place and purposing were crucial in all this. Home was important, and with it the home-team advantage. The rest of the house belonged to the Cabordets, of course. Fain's name was on the land certificate, replacing those of her parents. But the Star Dome didn't belong to Cass, it was *made* out of Cass, and it felt to Fain as though they might need that particular knife up their collective sleeve (not to neglect the other, actual, knife which she would bring tucked into her waist).

When I said I'd never open the Dome again, Cass says after a very long silence, *I wasn't just sulking.*

"I know that, Mum."

It's all bundled up in my mind with that time in our lives. I don't know if it will be the same now as it was. I don't know for sure that it will even be there. And if it is, there's no saying it will be safe. Or even stable. It might just break off, and then you'd all be stuck God-knows-where and I wouldn't have the strength in me to bring you back.

"I know there's a risk, Mum, but I think it's the only place where this has a chance of working. Aballach is the most powerful sorcerer any of us have ever seen—which makes sense, since he's stolen a lot of that power from all the demons he captured. But in the Star Dome he'll be having to push against *your* power. It gives us a kind of gradient that favours us. A bias. It might make all the difference."

Are you sure there's no other way?

"No," Fain says bluntly. "I'm only sure it's the best way. But there are other things we can try, and if you can't do this then you can't and there's an end of it. If you say no, I won't argue. I won't try to change your mind, I promise."

There's another silence, and again it goes on for a long while. Fain is about to point out that time is against them, that she needs an answer, when suddenly Cass speaks. *I was seeing if it was still there.*

"And?" Fain does her best to give the word a neutral inflection. There's no way on Earth she can make it as far as casual.

I can feel it. Almost as strong as in the old days. I think I can do it.

At that moment Mr Overton and Mr Henbosch return from their errand with a wheelbarrow full of metamorphosed demon. As soon as they're through the door there is no door. Instead there's Mina standing in the kitchen beside them as if she's been there all along. Which in a way, Fain reflects, she has.

"Where do you want this, Miss Cabordet?" Mr Overton asks.

"Follow me," Fain says.

They go out of the kitchen into the stairwell. The doors of the Star Dome open for them. Its strange light washes over them, its strange perfumes welcome.

"My word," Mr Overton exclaims.

"When is a door not a door?" Mr Henbosch asks rhetorically.

"Oh," Mina says, "almost always."

Like most people, Ortho Aballach is the hero of his own narrative. He sees himself as a paladin, leading a lone crusade against elemental evil. It's true that in order to do so he has to gloss over some of the more questionable uses to which he puts his wealth and power. He is a man who likes his pleasures, after all. Or as he puts it to himself, he has a lust for life. It's not blameworthy to enjoy the choicest fruits of civilisation, especially if you play a part in maintaining it.

In his memories, the epic battles he has fought against demonkind are constantly replayed. He is in awe of his own courage and virtuosity, of the force of his will and the works of his hands. He views his life in foreshortened perspective as an inexorable rise, a journey from nothing into something, a pilgrim's progress.

Yet paradoxically he has forgotten there was ever a time when his resources were scant and his victories came hard. He has become used to winning easily, inevitably. It has been many a long year since he fought in any meaningful sense for his life.

Esuluminax's escape filled him with rage and chagrin, but it did not make him re-appraise either his own strength or hers. He acknowledges that he made a mistake, underestimating the Brithual's resolution. It's not an error he intends to commit twice.

And Mrs Simons was only half-right when she speculated that Aballach chose his mode of entrance with drama in mind. There's another reason that weighs more heavily with him. The terms of his license allow him to force entry only if he is first refused it, so if he came to the front door he would be obliged to knock. To knock, and then to wait. That's not a thing he's prepared to contemplate.

So up onto the roof he goes, propelling himself by magics already written on his skin that make the law of gravity look the other way. Up to the roof and then down through the skylight. With the chromatophores in his suit turned all the way down to black he must look like some enormous bat. He flatters himself that he is terrifying.

He was expecting to find the house in darkness, the residents cowering behind locked doors. He is surprised to find that they are not only awake but active. From below, from the ground floor, comes a wash of light and a tinkling play of music. Trumpet. Clarinet. Trombone. String bass. The yawning boom of a big drum. A female voice sings, slow and sultry.

When the music comes around
Everybody goes to town
But there's something you should know…

The overall effect, Aballach decides, is artificial and dated. It's lounge jazz of another era, reinvented with enthusiasm but no real virtuosity. He curls his lip as he descends. It's not part of his remit but he'll put a stop to this while he's here, silence those instruments and that voice and do the whole neighbourhood a favour.

On the ground floor he finds himself facing a door that was not there on his earlier visit. This is far from surprising. He knows that Esuluminax will present as one of two things, a woman or a place, and even leaving that aside he can sense her. This morning the impression was faint and diffuse, but now it's intense and overwhelming and it's coming from directly ahead of him. He has found his quarry, and this will be even easier than he was expecting.

He makes to enter, but pauses for a moment on the threshold. The room that faces him is extraordinary, an assault on all his senses at once. Some kind of smoke machine has been deployed, filling the air with a thickly textured haze. The ceiling lamps are stars in an imagined firmament, but the light that's shed from them seems to drift down through the air as if it's in no particular hurry, changing colour as it goes. It paints the room rather than illuminating it. And it's perfumed. Each colour, inexplicably, has its own scent. The lights are bouquets, endlessly refreshed.

It's hard to say how big the room is, both because of the smoke or dust that's hanging in the air and because it's hard to make out the walls. They're skeins of smoke that take on the shifting hues of the lights and move with the rhythm of the music. There are tables all around the edges but the central space is a dance-floor. There are diners sitting at some of the tables but most of the clientele are up on the dance-floor, slow-dancing to the singer's louche, half-speed rendition of the Andrews Sisters' *Sing Sing Sing*. She's stationed at one end of the room behind an antique Radio City standing microphone, wearing a dress that's a vertical slash of crimson, shockingly vivid. Her black hair, worn short in a bob, has the gloss of a raven's wing. The band is up on a dais behind her. The suits they wear are sunset orange, russet red, wine-dregs purple. They have such wide lapels and such oversized buttons that they might as well be clown costumes. The drummer wears a fedora and has a cigarette dangling from the corner of his mouth. He runs a jazz brush over the top of the bass drum and grins at Aballach across the room.

All very elaborate, Aballach thinks. Smoke. Mirrors. Stage dressing. He refuses to engage with any of it.

"I'm here for Esuluminax," he calls out to the room at large. "I have a license to hunt her here and to take her directly into my custody. I mean to fulfil my brief, and as a direct consequence this is about to become a highly unstable environment. You should all leave by the nearest exit. I'd advise you do it in haste."

Nobody responds. The band keeps on playing, the dancers dance, the diners look up from their drinks but only for a moment, then they carry on with their conversations. The singer intones banalities into the mike. *Blow, blow, blow, blow. Listen to the trombones go! Baby there's something you should know…*

Aballach tries again. "The spell I'm about to cast," he says, raising his voice over the tinny clamour of the music and the singer's mumbling drawl, "will yank this entire room out of normal space and time and fold it down small enough for me to carry it away with me in my pocket. The side effects for anyone still present when that happens will be severe. I'll offer no further warnings."

At the end of this speech he can't hold back a cough. The air tastes gritty and slightly bitter. He needs to be done with this.

But there's still no reaction from anyone in the crowded room. It's as though he hasn't spoken. The soft light drifts down. The music plays. The gentle hubbub of the diners at the tables is undiminished. Who are all these people? When he came earlier in the day he encountered only three, the young hussy who manages the place and two of her down-at-heels boarders. Now he counts fifty or sixty, not including the band. Has this Cabordet woman invited the neighbours in to meet her resident demon? Has she turned a supernatural visitation into a side enterprise?

Aballach puts the question aside, swallows his vexation. Whatever she's done, it's no business of his—and he won't be to blame for any injury done to these people by what he's now required to do.

"Very well, then," he says grimly.

He summons his power and throws it outward, taking hold of the room by its edges and corners, preparing to gather its substance into a smaller compass and press it flat.

Or rather he tries, but the room evades his grasp. He finds he can't get any purchase on it at all. Which means...

Which means he must revise his appraisal of what's happening here.

Aballach squints his eyes and extends his senses. He could not have been mistaken about the demon's presence, but her location is another matter. The room, though magical in nature, is not her. She's somewhere else.

In fact, she's *everywhere* else. From outside the room he had felt a single focus, a strong and directional pull. Now, however, he's perceiving Esuluminax as being in front of him, behind him, surrounding him on all sides. There's not a thing here that doesn't seem to carry her mark, her effluvium. The dancers, the diners, the band, the singer, he stares at each in turn, studying face and form and features. Obviously if Esuluminax is not the room she must be *in* the room. It's logical to assume she's in human form, but in that case why is her spoor so widely spread? Where has she hidden herself, and how?

One of the diners stands. Aballach realises that he knows her. Though she's wearing some faded finery now, a cocktail dress in shades of blue and green with far too many frills and fripples, and though she's monstered her face with cheap cosmetics, this is the landlady. Cabordet. She folds her arms and meets his stare with insolent calm.

"You see?" she says. "We've got the measure of you, Mr Aballach. We don't particularly want to fight you, but we're not averse to the notion either. If you stay here you might find yourself being dealt with *summarily.*"

Aballach doesn't lower himself to bandying words with the landlady of a dilapidated seaside boarding house. His dignity is already imperilled here and it's incumbent on him not to give an inch. Wordlessly he scans Cabordet with the eyes of his spirit. She's perfused from head to toe with the demon's essence. At this point-blank range there's no mistaking it.

"Got you," Aballach snarls. Again he reaches out to claim what's his by right.

And again he's denied. Possibly the woman flinches a little when the magic touches her, but she doesn't fold inside out and shrink down to a nub. This is not Esuluminax in disguise. It's a mortal woman after all, although somehow she's allowed the demon's stink to rub off on her. No, to sink deeply into her.

Another woman sitting at the same table pushes back her chair and stands. She takes a swig of what looks to be whiskey and licks her lips. "Did you think you saw someone you knew, sweetheart?" she asks mildly. Esuluminax's essence is in her too, as strongly as in the Cabordet woman.

A pair of dancers wheels by. The woman grins over her shoulder, the mocking face all too familiar. Aballach lashes out, and his hand goes through her. It's a shock, but he rallies quickly. He thrusts his hand through a second dancer, then a third. All these cavorting couples are only conjured seemings. But the women are real, and that's useful to know. There are two magics here, one to flood the room with fakery and the other to spread the demon's spoor around the room and confuse his senses. Neither amounts to any more than a game of hide-and-go-seek, and neither will delay him long.

He makes a discreet gesture with his hand at the level of his waist. A breeze passes through the room, roiling the smoke in the air and ruffling the hair of some—but far from all—of the people he can see. It's gone in a few seconds, but its passage tells Aballach who here is real and who is false. They're all illusions, untouched by the fleeting gust, apart from the two women, a seated couple way over on his right, the singer and the drummer in the band.

Cabordet hasn't noticed his little experiment. She trails her fingers through the immaterial forearm of a handsome young man as he whirls by. Then she turns her back on Aballach as if he presents no threat at all and ambles across the room toward the stage. "My mother's charm," she calls over her shoulder. "One of the first she ever cast. Get people dancing by making them think people already are." Once she's reached the stage she doesn't step up onto it but turns again, fixing him with a look of cold insolence. "Would you care for a jig and reel, Mr Aballach?"

"No thank you," Aballach says. His throat catches, but he gets the words out. Only afterwards does he let loose another volley of coughs. He feels a little light-headed. The air here really is foul. As foul as the company. "You've wasted quite enough of my time. Give me the demon and a proper apology and I'll overlook the disrespect you've shown me."

"No," Cabordet says. "I don't think I'll do either of those things."

"Then you'll have to live with the consequences."

Aballach was on the brink of losing his temper, but now he's calm again. He has the situation entirely under control, despite all this unwieldy subterfuge. He approaches the stage, which is shallow enough to present no obstacle. He steps up beside the singer.

"You can't go there," Cabordet says from behind him.

Aballach pays her no mind. The singer is doing her best to pretend he isn't there, head bowed to one side as she murmurs languorously into the mike. "Just relax and take it slow, but sing, sing sing." He lifts up his hand and runs the tip of one finger along her cheek. It's solid flesh rather than airy nothing.

And she reeks of Esuluminax, but that no longer counts as proof. Nor does the way she flinches away as though his touch abrades her: it's a natural response to an unsolicited intimacy. He's almost sure, but he does what he needs to do to make that *almost* into a certainty. He raises up another tame wind. This time his gesture is more flamboyant, a little theatrical. Perhaps he's been infected by the atmosphere of this place (though it continues to vex his lungs and make his breathing stertorous).

He makes the wind buffet the singer, from one angle and then another. It creates holes and eddies in the haze, marking out a clear space around her as though it were a shepherd chivvying her away from her flock. It harries her sheer hair, forces her to close her eyes against its pressure. Finally it drives her long dress hard against her legs, rucking the fabric just enough to show her mismatched ankles.

One is of flesh. The other is made of wood.

"Esuluminax," Aballach says. "At longest last." And he lifts up his hand to perform the gesture that will unmake her.

In the back of his hand, between the second and third fingers, the hilt of a knife appears. He stares at it, utterly unable to fathom where it has come from. Then in quick succession he sees: Fain's hand, at the end of her fully extended arm, dropping from chin-height down to her waist; the expression of deep satisfaction on her face; the blade of the knife standing out from his palm where it has pierced him right through; the drummer whipping back the skin of the bass drum with a sudden flourish, and his own blood spattering down onto its rim.

It's not a drum at all. It's a *krater*, whose design Aballach recognises at once.

At longest last, sighs Achlys Mist of Sorrow.

This was always going to be the most precarious part of Fain's plan, which is perhaps best described not as a plan but as a number of moving parts in search of a shape.

Confusing Aballach's senses was her starting point, because it was the only thing about which she was tolerably confident. The opening of the Star Dome was a large part of that, being as it was a piece of reality belonging entirely to her mother. Aballach was used to making his own rules: here he would be subject to Cass's. It would be just a little harder for him to bring his powers to bear.

And Rosie had helped too, using her nursing skills and a borrowed transfusion kit from the Harbour Infirmary to share Mina's blood between the five of them. It wasn't really blood, of course, any more than Mina's flesh was flesh, but it would do as a medium for her Mina-ness. All of them would look and feel somewhat like her to Aballach's senses, which (Fain fervently hoped) would already be dulled by the unfamiliar ambience and her mother's active interference.

But a holding action only slows the guillotine blade, it doesn't stop it from falling. It was always inevitable that the binder would discover the dancers here were just decoy ducks, and that he only had six warm bodies to choose from.

Therefore, Fain's question to Achlys was as follows. "What if you were to drink of Aballach's blood?"

That would be joy beyond all joys. I would do anything—anything at all—for the chance to leave my mark on him.

"No, I mean, what would be likely to happen?"

Once I'd tasted of him, he would be in thrall to me, the demon said, with a hunger in her voice that was disconcerting. *It would give me dominion over his soul.*

"But you're already in thrall to him," Fain pointed out. "He's got dominion over you."

To my endless shame.

"So how would that resolve?"

Only silence from the vase.

"Achlys, I need to know what would—"

I cannot say. Such a thing has never happened.

"What, never? Not once? In all the ages that your kind and mine have shared the Earth together?"

If it happened, nobody spoke of it. I think it would twine his will and mine together into one thing. We would struggle, each against the other. Almost certainly the resolution of that struggle would end me, whether I win or lose. But I would hurt him in my passing, and in my passing I would be free of him.

Fain thought about this, weighing it against other matters already in train.

"You're sure?" she asks at last. "You're sure you'd risk even death to get out of this place?"

What's death but a pause in the music, long or short or everlasting? Only give me the chance!

"Good enough," Fain said. "I will, then."

And later, to Mr Henbosch, "Can you play the drums?"

"Not for a moment, Miss Cabordet."

"But can you *pretend* to play them?"

"With all my heart."

"Then in spite of my past strictures, Mr Henbosch, I need you to prepare a practical joke."

※

Now Aballach staggers, leaning backwards from his base as something rushes from the wine bowl's interior and hits him with solid force in his upper chest.

Solid force, but not a solid something. Whatever has grappled onto him is like the shadow cast by a candle flame, so faint and formless that it's almost not there at all. Still, it makes Aballach lurch and thrash the air, tottering on the balls of his feet as though he's about to launch into some complicated dance step.

Fain snatches up a second knife from one of the tables and moves in behind him, with Mina following a heartbeat later, but the binder sees them out of the corner of his eye. His middle finger twitches, and it's as though he's launched two simultaneous arrows from invisible bowstrings. Woman and demon are flung backwards off their feet.

But Aballach is struggling. His face is twisted in pain, his chest constricted by an unseen force. For a moment it seems as though he might really be in trouble. Then his fingers move again, pinching and flexing in synchrony, and all at once the candle flame goes out. A howl of rage and frustration shatters every glass in the room, and Achlys Mist of Sorrow is gone. Back into the wine bowl? Into some extra-dimensional void? Or is she just dead? There's no time right now to speculate. Aballach is still on his feet. Their first real shot has missed.

The second follows immediately. Mr Overton, who has remained seated all this time, now stands. He takes aim with his service weapon, which he has held folded in his lap. It's a bold and unexpected move, its strategic edge blunted only by a single factor. Unlike most revolvers the Webley-Fosbury has a manual safety, and Mr Overton would never dream of carrying the gun with the safety disengaged. There is an audible click before he pulls the trigger.

Aballach, forewarned, weaves another arabesque with his fingers. The gun bucks in Mr Overton's hand and the shot goes wide. But Mr Overton takes aim again, this time resting his right arm on his left to brace it.

He empties the Webley's magazine, which carries eight bullets rather than the more usual six. Aballach's fingers curl into claws, crimping the space between himself and the oncoming bullets. Then he opens them wide again, and reality convulses. Two bullets slam into the floor; three more are lost in the starlit void above; one shatters a drinking glass on a neighbouring table. The remaining one, the last one, stays on its right line, heading for Aballach's heart, but it slows and slows until its progress is a gentle dawdle.

Mina scrambles up from the floor and steps up behind the bullet. Bending from the waist she sets her lips to it and blows. It resumes its progress, accelerating. Seeing the threat, Aballach tries to speak a word of power. His lips move but his chest is clogged, his throat closing. The word does not emerge.

And the bullet doesn't stop. It hits Aballach just above his heart. It burrows its way in, slowly enough that all present can watch its progress.

The binder sways and lurches, sending the wine bowl rolling away across the floor. Surprise and dismay spread across his face. Once again he tries to speak, this time to pronounce a healing cantrip. Only a clotted gurgle comes from his lips.

"That's my mother again," Fain tells him. She waves her hand, disturbing the heavy haze that hangs in the air. "You've been breathing her in since you came into the room. A little of her, anyway. The human body after combustion yields up to six or seven pounds of ash, but I only kept as much as would fit in a jar."

Seems to have been enough to do the trick, though, Cass comments dryly.

Aballach's face is red as he tries to speak, and though he's having no luck with that his hands are busy too. There's no telling what other spells he might be weaving. "Out," Fain says. "Out of here. All of you, run."

And they do. Mr Henbosch has the best turn of speed out of all of them, Mrs Simons is slowest, but they all make it to the door. Fain risks one look over her shoulder. A fireball of immense proportions is forming in the air above Aballach's head. In its ferocious heat the microphone stand and the discarded instruments have already begun to melt.

Aballach points. The fireball breaks into a flood, a torrent of flame that rushes across the room towards them, devouring everything it touches.

Fain slams the doors shut. The line between them glows for a moment with unearthly radiance. Mina takes hold of her, folds her in a tight embrace and turns her back to the doors, putting her own body between Fain and the fire.

But there is no fire. In that instant the closed doors have vanished. The wall is whole again, unbroken.

They're all silent for a moment as they digest this fact. "Where..." Mr Henbosch essays. "Where is Mr Aballach now?"

"Wherever music goes," Fain says, "when it's not being played."

The Star Dome is now closed, Cass Cabordet declares with suitable gravitas. *Thank you all for joining us for this very special farewell evening.*

※

They go back to their lives, which for the most part are lying where they left them.

Fain is expecting at least one or two of her boarders to give in their notice after such perturbing events, but to her surprise and relief nobody does. "Why would they?" Mina asks her. "This is their home, Fain. They love it here."

And they do. Of course they do. Even in Hove Harbour, which fervently embraces difference, there's no other boarding house that's quite like this one. No other where the floor plans change at night, and where any door opened at random might reveal your heart's desire.

But Mina means more than that. As she told Fain once before, the places we love are the places where we're strongest. And the Ocean View has a strength all its own, being not one house at all but two houses that have fallen in love and married.

Fain and Mina haven't taken that particular step—marriage—but it's not because they have any doubts about their love for one another. It's only that Mina doesn't put any particular stock in promises made in a church. She feels that she and Fain pledged to each other in that kitchen, when Fain rejected Aballach's bribe and swore to protect her against anything or anyone that came to take her.

In any event, the first-floor seaward front room is hers now as well as Fain's. Cass (no longer confined to an urn since her ashes were scattered in another dimension) lives mostly in the downstairs lounge but also makes frequent visits to the cinema, the Red Curtain cabaret and even further afield. She has dropped hints to the effect that some day soon she may go as far as Heaven and see for herself what it's like. She feels she might actually be ready now, having seen her only daughter settled at last.

Fain and Mina go travelling sometimes too. It's no hard thing at all for the daughters of Lilith's daughters to move from one reality to the next as if all those distant worlds were only the chalked squares on a pavement hopscotch court. Fain has seen wonders beyond imagining; the ruins of Sheppanupshet, the Tears of God at Lian Tau, the migration of the mountain giants, the stepped cities of the Arkior, the spider roads of Woerpin, the centaurs dancing in the Spring on the slopes of Parnassus. Her old wanderlust is pampered and indulged beyond anything she could ever have imagined.

And she's popular in those other realms. The daughters of Lilith's daughters, set free by their sister Esuluminax after Aballach's fall, have sung to all and some the praises of Josephine Cabordet, the seaside landlady who measured might with the hated binder and breaker, and bound him and broke him. There are parties in her honour in fields of gold and palaces of stardust.

But no matter how far she goes and what wonders she sees, there's always a lightness in Fain's heart when she turns for home. She knows for certain now where it is she belongs, and that's a blessing in itself.

Acknowledgements

"Thanks are due to editor supreme Marie O'Regan and to Pete and Nicky for letting me be a part of this. Thanks also to my agent, the awesome Meg Davis. Thanks above all to my beta readers, Lin and Lou, who gave me precious feedback, and to my sons, Davey and Ben, who gave me equally precious support."